Different

Strokes

www.barbarianspy.com

This book is copyright © habu 2017
habu asserts his right to be known as the author of this work.
Published by BarbarianSpy in 2017
Cover design © S Bush 2017
Cover image: BarbarianSpy
ISBN: E-Book: 978-1-925568-29-5
Paperback: 978-1-925568-30-1
All rights reserved

BarbarianSpy
Toronto, Australia

Different

Strokes

Habu

Table of Contents

Introduction

Keith Evans and Tyler Sinclair are near twins in near identical situations. They both are young, handsome blond surfers finding themselves set down on the remote American-territory island of Guam and on their own. They both are fine with and good with sex with men and are keeping their lives together by being lower-price rent-boys in the Tumon area of the island for sailors coming off the naval ships on shore leave.

They both are hired by a sex industry high roller for a fashion show modeling job, their services being auctioned off to attendees at the show, and the job includes a paid appearance in a porn movie. The opportunity presents the possibility of opening doors into higher-class male prostitution for both of them. Each, in turn, is offered a week's trip to Hawaii as a full-sexual-services escort companion to a randy and demanding Korean businessman engaged in landing a hush-hush business deal. From here the two take very different paths, Keith in "Free Spirit" and Tyler in "Aloha Week." Will their "different stroke" decisions have very different results?

Free Spirit

We were getting to the main event. Sailor A was lying on his back on the hotel room bed, legs dangling over the foot of the bed, and I was sitting on his cock, facing the foot of the bed. Sailor B was standing in front of me, his hands holding my head, and I was giving him head, while, using the leverage of my feet digging into the edge of the mattress and in a crouch on the bed on either side of Sailor A's thighs, I rose and fell on Sailor A's cock, fucking myself. Sailor A was just lying there, his hands loosely on my waist, but not doing anything but holding his hard. I would have liked him to be a little more active. He was the cute one of the pair.

I clutched Sailor B's butt cheeks to keep myself steady. I didn't often do two-for-ones. I was doing that now, though. I'd given them a high price half thinking they'd back off, but they didn't. That was the thing with the sailors. They came off the ships horny and ready to go, but often without enough cash to give it a really good go.

They'd given me their names, but damned if I could remember them. This was their hotel room, at the Ypao Breeze Inn in Tumon, the touristy resort area on the west coast of Guam. It wasn't exactly a dive, but it wasn't the Ritz either. I could fuck on this bed—and I usually did when ships were in at the naval base—but I was glad I didn't have to sleep on it. I wondered if both of the sailors would be sleeping on it—and if they had sex with each other. Maybe they were in the room only long enough to use me in shore leave relief, and they'd go back on their ship after they'd done me. They certainly were royally doing me. Maybe I hadn't asked for enough money. I kept forgetting that the sailors arrived revved up and full of cum and could fuck like bunnies.

Both sailors were muscular. Both had average-sized cocks. One was younger and good-looking in a full-lipped, sultry way. The other was older, pretty ugly in the face, but having the better muscle definition of the two in the body, probably because he was more mature and more wiry. They'd told me the name of the ship they'd come off for shore leave from the naval base further south on the coast, but I hadn't remembered that either. Nor did I remember the name of the guy who had given them my telephone number for the hookup.

Some things were important to remember. For repeat sailors I could look at the face and know the size of his cock and how he used it. What was going on here wasn't that important. This was just paying the bills to cover what I really was on Guam to do—to ride the surf and paint. That's what was important to me. I was highly sexed, though, and had to have it regularly. Laying down for the sailors and being paid to do it scratched a couple of my itches.

Sailor B, the older guy, was the active one here, telling and showing me what they wanted me to do for them. Sailor A seemed to be along for the ride, more interested in Sailor B and pleasing him than in me, which was a pity because he aroused me in ways the older one didn't.

Sailor B fucked me as soon as we got in the room, bending me over the bed after I'd stripped for them and knelt in front of them, with them arm in arm, and worked them hard together, taking them both in my mouth at the same time as I was able. Sailor B ate my ass out as I was bent over the bed, fingered me for a minute or so, snapped a rubber on, slapped his cock around on my buttocks a few times, ran it over the hole, and then was inside me, pumping and snorting. Sailor A sat in the room's desk chair, beat his meat, and watched the action, egging Sailor B on with words that had a nervous edge to them. He wasn't comfortable doing this. Sailor B was very comfortable doing this.

Sailor B was efficient and straightforward and went directly for an initial jack off. They'd paid for multiples and a special, so I knew this was just Sailor B getting his anticipation rocks off—that he'd take it slower and more deliberately in subsequent rounds. I wouldn't have minded if Sailor A, the cute one, took up position behind me after the ugly one pulled out, but he didn't. They sat side by side on the foot of the bed and I knelt in front of them and handed and sucked on their cocks again.

They leaned into each other and kissed while I worked on their cocks, and that answered the "what are they to each other?" question for me. They probably were a couple on the ship, with older Sailor B seeing it as getting-his-rocks-off sex and cuter Sailor A seeing it as love. The cute one was here only because the older one wanted the variety with a rent-boy—with a third party they didn't have to live with on the ship.

When we moved into the "special," the cuter, younger guy just lay under me with his cock up my ass and moving it slightly in countermotion to my rises and

11

falls. Sailor B, who I'd been sucking off, took the root of his cock and pulled it out of my mouth. He lowered his face to mine and took my mouth with his in a kiss. I felt him frotting our cocks together and stroking them. I continued rising and falling on Sailor A's cock. I felt that Sailor B was working toward the special—the double—though, and I was right.

This wasn't a favorite of mine, but they'd paid for it and I'd agreed to it. Neither of them was hung. I could manage them. It was something I was pleased to have managed—after it was over and the money for it had exchanged hands.

Sailor B was pressing on my chest with his free hand, and I arched back into Sailor A's chest, whereupon Sailor A wrapped his arms around my chest to hold me there. I groaned and opened my mouth in a wide yawn, which was the alternative to crying out, which I didn't really want to do in a hotel with paper-thin walls, as Sailor B worked his cock into my ass above Sailor A's cock. I did let out an "Oh, shit. Oh, fuck," though. I knew they'd want to think they were putting me in on-the-edge distress.

I gasped, gulped in air, and gave them a strained, "Oh fuckin' fuck. Shit, shit, shit," as Sailor B bottomed and began a slow pump.

It was only painful for a few minutes. My passage was well used, and I knew the tricks of relaxing and willing the passage to stretch. It had taken a variety of sizes and it had doubled for bigger cocks than this. The walls stretched to take them and rippled over both cocks, inviting them both to stroke. That was a special feeling when both cocks of a double were actively stroking. That wasn't the case here. Sailor A held steady, his cock throbbing inside me and him moaning as Sailor B stroked his cock slowly inside me. I just concentrated on being as relaxed and open as possible.

"Like that, do you?" Sailor B whispered in my ear, and I voiced a dutiful, "Yes, yes. Yes! Fuck me!"

Happily, it didn't take either long for both of them to fill out the bulbs of their condoms.

They lay on their sides on either side of me, touching me here, there, everywhere, intimately. Sailor A, more demonstrative now, touched me on my inner thighs and stroked them. I spread them and put a leg over the legs of the sailor on either side of me and planted my feet on the other side of them. "Raise your tail," Sailor B commanded, and when I did he, bolder than the cute one, had fingers up my ass.

"Come for us," Sailor B directed, and there, with my legs over theirs and raising my pelvis off the mattress, I stroked off my cock. They both exclaimed their pleasure when I shot off in a strong arc of cum. Sailor B continued playing with my cock after I'd ejaculated and lowered my tail again.

"Like this?" he murmured.

"Um, um," I sighed in affirmative, knowing that was what he wanted to hear, although I did like it—and would have liked it better if Sailor A was doing it. I was built bigger than either of them, and Sailor B seemed to enjoy the size of me and making me fill out. While he fondled me, he licked my cum off my belly, and exchanged cum-laced saliva with me in a kiss. I got the impression that he missed some of the kinkier aspects of sex—that it wasn't something that turned Sailor A on, so rent-boy sessions like this when they got into port were meant to rev up Sailor B's engines.

I also got the hint from his playing with my cock that maybe he went both ways. Maybe he'd want me or

Sailor A to spike *him* before the evening was over. Maybe *he* wanted to be doubled and was building up to that.

They weren't finished. They'd paid enough not to be finished. They lay on the bed, shorter Sailor A stretched out on top of taller Sailor B, Sailor B's cock poking through under Sailor A's scrotum, and, kneeling below them, I sucked off both cocks, together, unhinging my jaw to take both of them in. They liked that. They obviously liked having both of their cocks engaged together.

Sailor B fulfilled my suspicion for the finale. He rolled me onto my back on the bed, jacked me hard with his hand, crowned my cock, climbed on top of me, and moved into the saddle, positioning my cock head at his hole, sitting on it, and sliding down the pole. He rode my cock while Sailor A lay beside us on bed, watching his partner milk my cock with his passage muscles, conveying in his eyes that it would have been quite all right with him for them to have kept the hotel room to themselves, with him, rather than me, fucking Sailor B.

That was OK with me—that the sailor was using my cock. I was versatile and didn't get many clients who wanted me to fuck them. Other than the oversized cock, I was built to be a submissive—slightly less than average height; a willowy body, although muscled up enough to please the eye; smooth, hairless torso; slim hips, flat belly and plump buttocks; trimmed pubes; androgynous features that were assessed more to be beautiful than handsome; watery blue eyes and blond hair with platinum highlights that I kept shoulder length and had in a ponytail except during sex. Men liked to run their fingers through my hair during sex—

or, if they were thuggish, to use my hair as a handle to drag me around with. Either way, they could excite me.

It was my seven thick inches hard that surprised, although I wore clothes tailored to give a hint of it. And I didn't usually wear underwear at all. That really turned the johns on, seeing me in the raw when I unzipped and flared my shorts, giving them a shot of the trimmed golden curlies followed by the root of a thick cock. Often they stopped me there and took out their cell phones to take a photo to take home with them. I didn't care. I wasn't ashamed of my package, and it wasn't a head shot.

They were both off the bed after Sailor B had fucked himself on my cock and headed for the shower. I heard sounds of them fucking in the shower. It sounded like it was the younger guy, Sailor A, who was fucking Sailor B, which is what I thought he longed to do the whole time.

I lay there watching them as they dressed. They'd counted out $400 and put it on the dresser, so unless there was any last-minute funny business, we were all good. That was a lot of money for a sailor trick, although it was two of them. They both had great bodies, which I guessed was usual for working sailors. It was why I liked to lay down for the sailors rather than working the businessmen of Tumon. It was just that, although it was only a business transaction, I would have liked Sailor A to have more actively fucked me. It wasn't a bad way to earn $400, though. It wouldn't have been nearly that much without the DP. I had three days of abstinence coming up, so the money was welcome.

Sailor B turned to me. "The bathroom's all yours now if you want to clean up. If you'll show us a good

15

bar for us to go, we'll stand you a drink. You did great. If you have a card we'd be happy to pass it on."

It was 10:00 p.m., a good time to go cruising. They'd stood me a steak dinner before we'd come up to the hotel room. They had fucked me—and each other—for more than an hour and a half and paid me well for it. I couldn't see any reason not to steer them to a good club for the rest of the night.

I took them to Denial, which was nearby and which had a good band going, a dance floor, pool tables, and a bar. They could pick their interest. Since their ship was in, they hooked up there with some of their mates. They ordered me a drink and paid for it, I gave each of them my card, and they went off to the pool tables while I leaned against the bar and contemplated whether I could—or wanted to—fit in another john that night. The ship had just come in, so there was no doubt that I could pick someone up for an energetic hour in the hay. Was I up for energetic, though? I checked my mind and ran a mental scan for aches and pains and was surprised to learn that I was up for nasty.

I would have to go three days after this without turning a trick. I'd enjoy the time off to do what I came to Guam to do, but the money would have to stretch. I'd made good money for a day, and I usually worked only long enough to feed my surfing and painting habit for the foreseeable future. I lived up the coast near Fai Fai Beach, on a more quiet stretch of the South Marine Corps Drive coast road, and I only came into Tumon when I needed to replenish the cookie jar. My Jeep Wrangler was ancient and I didn't exercise it any more than I had to.

There was a clean-cut, good-looking guy who obviously wasn't Navy—more professional or businessman—sitting at a table across the room and looking at me. I looked back, instantly attracted to him, even though my mind check had come back "nasty," and this guy didn't look like that's what he was looking for. I was concentrating on thuggish sailors, who fucked fast—if furiously and multiple times—and who would be on a ship again before they could complicate my life with claims of commitment. A guy in civvies might be a permanent resident and come with issues that didn't want to go away easily.

The guy was maybe in his early forties, but strikingly good looking and solid, and, regardless of the "local john" possible problems, I was thinking of maybe going over and asking him if he'd like some company. Before I could do so, though, there was a chunky hunky sailor at my elbow dropping one of the cards that I had just given out to Sailors A and B on the bar top. "Chunky hunky" is a name I give to big bruisers who would be considered overweight if they weren't so massive that they carried the weight more as muscle than as excess padding.

He looked thuggish and would, by my guess, give me a cruel ride. But part of why I chose to make my money this way was that I liked variety and was turned on by a little danger and manhandling. I didn't object to being knocked around a bit occasionally. Sometimes the vanilla sex dulled my arousal. Being taken by a thug now and then sharpened my appetite for it. Of course I didn't need the sex—or so I kept telling myself—but as long as I was in that business, it was good to sharpen the arousal now and then.

He was interested and he had the money. He also would pay for the room but only at a cheap motel. I took him back to the Ypao Breeze Inn, which was nearby. Once in the room, he was impressed that just an unzip and tug on the hips of my trousers had me ready for him. He slapped me around, did me in a doggie on the floor, slapped me around some more, tossed me on the bed and, with a massive cock, brutalized me with a pistoning missionary accompanied by a choke hold with a strong, calloused, Navy man's hand. He left me moaning and with my legs spread wide for some time to come. But he did leave me with the room for the rest of the night and left the agreed amount of money on the desk.

In this business, you take the bad with the good—the brutal with the vanilla. And without some manhandling thrown in, you could too easily become numb to it. I was a rent-boy not only because it was a relatively easy way to make money on Guam if you were good-looking, trim, and submissive. I was a rent-boy because I enjoyed having a man's cock inside me.

My dwelling was not much more than a shack on a beach near Fai Fai Beach—one large room with a floor-to-ceiling glass window to take advantage of the light for my painting. I managed to haul out of the hotel early enough next morning that I was back at my place in time to grab a couple of fried eggs and be wading out into the surf with my board as the sun was coming up. I surfed for an hour, first alone but increasingly with buddies who showed up here regularly to take the waves. When I returned to the beach, I could see that the retired sergeant, Sid Tanner, who was in a wheelchair and who owned one of the small houses with a large deck on the hill overlooking the beach, was out, watching me.

We had an arrangement. I went up the beach and climbed the wooden stairs to his deck. As the sun climbed up in the sky, I sat, facing him, on his cock in his wheel chair, and rode him to his ejaculation while he licked and sucked on my nipples and whispered his thanks over and over again. It was about the only excitement he got twice a week and he paid for the Wi-Fi in my shack. Beyond that, I considered it a thanks for his service to the nation. He lost use of the legs in Afghanistan; I saw no reason why that should be rewarded by losing use of his cock before he had to. I wasn't a totally selfish shit.

I liked this regular fuck almost as much as Sid did. I couldn't reach the deck with my feet with my legs hanging over the wheel chair arms, so it gave my thighs muscles and my biceps exercise in rising and falling on his cock. He was paralyzed down there except for his cock, which was capable of erection, of feeling the rub, and of ejaculating. He had what they called a beer can cock—all thickness and little length. That too was an aid to me in training my hole to be able to open quickly and wide. My hole, like the rest of my body, was deceptively small until it had received a thick cock or two. It was part of the turn-on for some johns—that what I had to receive them with looked like it couldn't manage them, but that it then did—swallowed them right up to the short hairs, rippled over them, and milked them dry. It was a talent, and it put money in the bank.

Returning home, I painted for two hours, this being the best day for the angle of the light coming into my essentially one-room—although it was a big room—abode, and then I slept for four hours.

Just another day of filling in and paying for the days of a free spirit on the island of Guam. I didn't apologize for the prostitution. I had a young, supple body, a talented hole and passage, and a good face that men lusted after. And it was my life to do with as I liked. I wasn't so invested in it—I didn't think I needed cocking as much as I made use of it to support my free and easy lifestyle—that I couldn't give it up when my paintings started to sell well. They sold now—just not well.

* * * *

At 11:00 I was at the free clinic on South Marine Corps Drive that I'd been sent to for a blood test. I tested for HIV regularly anyway, but this was a special. If I cleared, which I did, and abstained for the next three days after the test, I could do a one-day, one-night $1,000 gig at a private ocean-side mansion north of Tumon. The owner of the mansion, a mixed Japanese-American named Lee Houser, was a sometimes client of mine—he usually went for higher-drawer hookers than I was and ones he could certifiably bareback, which I couldn't afford to accommodate in normal circumstances, but sometimes, he said, he liked to go with someone less practiced and jaded. He also hung nearly a foot long hard, which required some recovery time afterward but was oh-so melting in view of what a guy managed to sheath. When he did me, I usually just lay there, willing myself to open, breathing shallowly, whimpering, and concentrating on how far up into new territory he was journeying—giving a long sigh as he withdrew it and a deep gasp as he slid it in deep again—and then again and again.

It was a test of how much pain a guy was willing to endure for the high of knowing he'd taken something that big and of just how much a submissive wanted cock. He convinced me I wanted cock.

He had a friend who was a men's fashion designer and another one who shot porno films, and he was doing a combination day. One of his regular models was AWOL, given to accepting offers of week-long jaunts to Hawaii or Australia, and I was offered a last-minute fill in slot—for $1,000, plus any tips I got. That would do me for more than a month of living my way on Guam.

While I was waiting for the test, my attention went to a white-coated doctor walking across a doorway to the clinic's examination rooms. I might not have noticed him if he hadn't stopped in mid walk and stared at me. It was the man who had been at the table across the room at Denial the previous night—the man I'd established "you're interesting" eye contact with before the bruiser took me back to the Ypao Breeze Inn and humped me into submission.

He came out into the waiting room, but he didn't come over to me. He had a short conversation with one of the receptionists, but he kept looking my way. When I left after taking the test—but not seeing him again when I was back in the guts of the clinic—I stopped at the receptionist and asked who he was.

"Dr. Prentice," she said, cheerily. "Dr. Paul Prentice. He's the senior doctor here. Do you need to make an appointment to see him? Were you referred."

"No, thanks," I said. "I just thought I'd seen him before."

"Probably in the papers. He does a lot of work with charities."

Charities. That's what Lee Houser was running the fashion show at his house for—for a free gay man's clinic in the slums of Tumon. The porn filming later in the day wasn't acknowledged anywhere in the publicity. Nor was it acknowledged that an hour with each of the models was being auctioned off, although Houser said that money was going to the clinic too. In fact, it was the bulk of the money the clinic would get. The models would get 25 percent of the auction price.

So, three days later—three delightful days of surfing and painting, one of the paintings coming out to be a nude of my vision of Dr. Paul Prentice—I was at Houser's multimillion dollar house hanging out over the ocean on a cliff north of Tumon and modeling tuxes, suits, casual wear, beach wear, and, last, micro thongs best suited for the bedrooms of a bordello. There were four of us who were walking the runway— two smaller guys, including me, and two muscled-up hunks. The other smaller guy, Tyler, was a near duplicate of me—small, blond, willowy, androgynous, slim hipped, and sexy, if I do say so myself.

He was not for me, of course, as it was obvious we swung the same way. I'd seen him at the beach before, riding a board, same as me. I had been told the four of us would pair up for the porno films later in the day. I eyed the two muscular guys, trying to figure out which one would be mine. They were both body and face beautiful. One looked more dangerous than the other, though. It could have been because he was part Chinese and had a colorful dragon-scene tattoo that covered his left breast, around to his shoulder blade, and down his left arm to his elbow.

The catwalk was out on the wide, deep deck hanging out over the cliff head. The walkway came out of a bedroom at one end of the house—where we changed—and went around in front of the living room, dining room, and kitchen, and entered into a den, from whence we ran back across the interior of the house to the bedroom to change for the next pass.

The buyers, having been fed lunch, came out onto the deck and sat in chairs strung down between the cat walk and the railing overlooking the ocean.

Dr. Prentice was there. That threw me for a loop when I first came out, in a tuxedo, and passed by him on the catwalk. But then, while I changed for the suit walk, I reasoned that that made sense. I figured he was gay. I'd seen him at Denial, and we'd shared gazes of unmistakable interest. The interest was there in his eyes at the clinic three days previously as well. And he was a doctor and was known to support charities. This was a charity event for a clinic. It aroused me to see him there, in the audience, but I had a job to do, money to earn, and I settled down to trying to do the modeling as professionally as the others did.

A walrus of a man in his late fifties won me in the auction of models. I was thrilled to see that Prentice bid on me—and none of the other guys—although he dropped out when the expense got into nosebleed territory. The walrus bidder fucked me—or rather, I rode his cock—on the bed in an upstairs bedroom, with the windows open to the sound of the angry surf below the cliff.

He lay there like a beached whale, not really gross other than his rotund stomach, and, for starters, I lay below him, between his spread legs, and sucked his cock, which was presentable, and played with, sucked, and distended his huge balls, which were interesting enough that, stroking myself at the same time, they enabled me to harden so that, when I moved up his body and saddled over his chest, my butt resting on the great mound of his stomach, I was able to convince him I was aroused as he took my cock in his mouth and sucked me to an ejaculation, which he willingly and happily took in his throat.

I gave him what would pass as a sexy massage then, kneading his muscles, of which he did have some, no doubt maintained on the golf course, and his rolls of fat, and stroking his cock hard again. To his sighs and moans, I mounted his hips, facing away from him, took him inside me, and, gripping his knees with my hands and arching my torso over his thighs, rode his cock to his barebacking completion. then I leaned down and licked his legs and ankles until he had rehardened and I rode him again. He was virile for an out-of-shape man in his fifties. I didn't know if I could pull a third ejaculation out of him in the hour, but I did—and he produced a prodigious wad of cum each time.

I didn't know what his winning bid had been in the auction until the accounting came in later and I'd earned an extra $150—which meant he had bid $600 for my services—but he left the bedroom happy, leaving me a $50 tip. Houser had passed the word to treat him right, no matter what, and have him leave happy. I was more interested in making Houser happy, so I did what I could.

The walrus asked for my card, so chances were good I was adding a big spender to my client list. For an even $500, I'd let a whale fuck me.

I had pulled the tattooed part-Chinaman for my porn film partner that evening, which was fine with me. The movie was filmed in an upstairs bedroom of the cliffside mansion. Ours was the second of two sessions. Tyler was still lying on his back on the bed, legs open, arms akimbo, and looking dopey and well worked over when I arrived. His hole was gaping and leaking cum. A couple of guys were standing there, holding sheets and waiting for Tyler to come to enough to vacate the bed so that they could change the sheeting when the half-Chinese guy, who was named William, and I were taking our instructions on what the scene would be.

My film partner pointed to Tyler and laughed. "See that," he said. "I'm going to leave you as fucked silly as that guy is."

I laughed at his joke, but it wasn't a joke, and he did just that, although he came at it from a different angle. Tyler looked like he'd been brutalized. On the whole, the half-Chinese guy loved me to death.

The scene described to us had almost no plot, of course, but, in spite of our disparate sizes and perhaps for the surprise of it, it was to be a romantic scene. The director of the film, half something black, trouserless, and his dong erect, probably from a successful earlier filming, gave us direction in a half pant and told us to get right to it. "Just leave the little guy well fucked," he said.

"No problem," my film partner responded.

"If I don't think you've fucked him good enough, I'll do it myself." the director said.

"You'll do it anyway, won't you?" the big guy shot back.

"Probably," answered the director. "It's the second shoot. So I can shoot when it's done. They saved the cutest one for last." They both laughed. I didn't particularly like them standing there talking about me like I wasn't standing there too, so I didn't join in the laughter.

We entered the room in the thong swimsuits from the fashion show and with towels over our shoulders, like we'd just come from the pool. We opened with standing kissing and petting. William pressed down on my shoulders and I knelt in front of him and gave him prolonged head. His cock was very nice. He gently laid me on the foot of the bed, my legs dangling down to the floor and spread, and spent several minutes while the video whirred eating my ass out and finger fucking it with good camera angles, while he sucked me. We did a couple of minutes of sixty-nining on the bed, him stretched over me, and then he took me in his arms, maneuvered me into a position where the camera could get a prolonged shot of his thick cock invading and conquering my puckering, small hole, showing me opening to the thick shaft, and then he fucked me for twenty minutes in positions that showed his domination but also highlighted the romantic pleasure we both were getting from the fuck.

William was an expert at porn films. I wasn't, but I was totally submissive to him, which is what I understood was wanted, and I think I did fine.

The director must have thought I did fine too, because when the end of the shot was announced, with both William and me on our backs, beside each other, shooting our loads one after the other, and William had rolled off the bed, the director came onto the bed, separated my thighs with his hands, hunched over me, thrust inside me with his big black cock, and pistoned me to his release. He didn't ask my permission. I wanted to impress Houser, so I didn't make any waves. To the director, I'm sure, porn actors were just slabs of meat to be consumed when and as they wished.

He wasn't anything close to being as gentle as William was with me, but bouncing around in the bed under the director, meeting his thrusts with countermotions with my pelvis, I met him heat for heat.

I did like to be barebacked when that was in the cards, and I had been barebacked by three nice cocks—a white one, a half Chinese one, and a black one. And I was being paid more than a month's worth of support in one day too.

The next morning I came awake in a big bed in yet another of the mansion's bedrooms. The windows were open and I wakened slowly to the sound of the surf below. As a devoted surfer, I could hear no more pleasant sound than that of the surf meeting the shore. I was sore, but I was satisfied.

Lee Houser was standing at one of the windows, looking out at the ocean. He was smoking a reefer and had a mug of steaming coffee in his hand. He had a silk kimono on his back, but it was open, showing a lean, well-muscled physique. Two more mugs were on a tray on a nightstand next to the bed. I didn't know why there would be two, but I didn't give it much thought. They both were steaming now, apparently having just been delivered by one of the Filipino servants who padded around Houser's mansion, but I figured it would be cold before I could get to it.

Houser's nearly foot-long, relatively thin cock was sticking out in full erection.

"Ah, good, Keith. You're awake."

I spread and bent my legs, stuffing a pillow under the small of my back as he put the smoke and coffee mug down on the nightstand, shrugged off his kimono, and climbed up on the foot of the thick-mattressed bed. He hovered over me, propped up by stiffened arms on either side of my shoulders and smiled down into my face, as he started the long, long, long slide into me. I grasped his shoulder blades in my hands and gasped and gulped as he possessed me as no other man had done, sinking deep into my gut—nearly twelve inches of throbbing, raw-skinned cock. The muscles of my walls were going wild again—he had fucked me at least three times during the night; I had passed out at one point—fighting to close up on the relatively thin cock, rippling over the flesh-on-flesh shaft, grasping and squeezing it and pulling it deep inside me. I moaned deeply, moving my hands to grasping his buttocks, as he began to pump, deep, deep inside me. Allowing my head to turn to the side, cheek to pillow, I opened my mouth in a gaping yawn; my eyes glazing over; panting lightly, moaning deeply; and reveled in a slow, deep fuck that no john had ever been able to give me before. My walls had struggled to spread open to a man before, but they were equally exercised to close on and undulate over the long, thin one.

Slow thrust up into my gut; shuddering thrust of my pelvis down to meet it. Slow thrust up into my gut . . .

28

There were times when I was an in-control, cynical rent-boy. This wasn't one of those times. For this time I was a small, young man, covered by an experienced, masterful man with an impossibly possessive monster cock and being laid out and totally fucked—for the fourth time in the span of eight hours. And Houser knew it. He held there, hovering over me, having released his seed deep inside me for the fourth time, my cum slathered on his body, and looked down into my eyes, his smile almost a leer. He knew he had conquered me, that I had surrendered fully to him, that I was his slave to use as he wished.

"Turn over," he said. "Turn over and go up on your knees."

"Enough. No more," I whined.

"Turn over. Turn over and go up on your knees," he repeated.

Groaning, almost sobbing, I rolled out from underneath him, went up on my knees, my cheek pressed to the pillow, my arms straight out from my sides in a cruciform form of surrender, and, crouching over me like a horse jockey, he mounted my hips, invaded my ass, and began the dance of the fuck again.

It was one of the few times I've been fully satiated, but it scared the beezeeges out of me. I had become a rent-boy with the understanding that I could maintain control, that I didn't need the sex, that I could hold myself above it all, do it but not be controlled or consumed by it.

I groaned as he slid inside me again, deep, pressed his fists into my shoulder blades to keep my chest flat on the bed and once more began to pump. Tears came to my eyes in the realization that I wanted him inside me—needed him inside me.

About the time it struck me that I'd been the one chosen to spend the night under him, memory clicked in. It hadn't been just me, which explained the additional cup of coffee. The other small blond from the fashion show, Tyler, came out of an adjacent bathroom and climbed up on the bed, stretching out beside me, but at a distance, as it was a huge bed. Houser turned from me to Tyler. His hand went between Tyler's thighs, and he coaxed them open.

"Push your hips up for me, baby," Houser murmured, and when Tyler did, Houser rolled over between his legs, spiked his ass and began to pump him. Tyler turned his face to me, giving me a glassy, "He's inside me now" stare.

I rolled out of the other side of the bed and went for a shower, taking one of the mugs of now-tepid coffee with me.

I went home $1,400 richer—Houser had sweetened the pot by $200 and promised to use me as a model again—and went straight to bed and slept through the day. I was up before dawn the next day, though, and out in the surf—just me and the ocean—with memories of that foot-long cock churning inside me. I was sore as hell deep inside—and the soreness wasn't all physical. Moving with the high-rollers was hard work.

* * * *

Maria, my Filipina cleaning lady, who I splurged to have not only because, although I appreciated neatness, I was incapable of sustaining neatness myself but also because I enjoyed the normalcy of her company in my solitary life, had arrived at the shack and was cleaning. She was intensely cleaning, which wasn't like her. And her greeting had been perfunctory.

"What's wrong, Maria?" I asked. You're not yourself today.

"It's not your concern, Mr. Evans," she said, her words clipped.

"Have I done something to upset you?"

"No, no, of course not. You aren't like those other whites."

"What other whites?"

"Like that retired Navy officer who lives in that big house down the road. The one who, with his wife and all of their bratty children, think they are better than anyone else."

"What have they done now?"

"Ferdinand. Their pool man. One of the Filipino community. They fired him."

"Fired him? What did he do wrong?"

"He fell by their pool and busted up his arm."

"Did they take him to the doctor?"

"No, they fired him. Told him to get out. He left holding his arm, as I was coming to work. I got him a taxi to go back to his house."

"He didn't go to a doctor?"

"He can't afford a doctor here. Doctors are for snotty white people like that retired Navy officer."

"Where is he, Maria?"

"At his big house down the street, probably. Swimming in his big pool. I think they wanted an excuse to fire Ferdinand, because he's gotten old."

"No, I mean, Ferdinand, Maria. Where is Ferdinand?"

"At home probably. Putting ice on his arm."

31

"He may need more than ice. Come on. Get in the Jeep. We'll go check his condition out."

An hour and a half later we—Maria, Ferdinand, and I—were at the free clinic on South Marine Corps Drive. Paul Prentice was the doctor who came out to take a look at the arm. He did a bit of a double take when he saw that I was with Ferdinand and Maria.

"What seems to be wrong?" he asked, looking somewhere between the three of us rather than at Ferdinand, standing there holding an obviously broken arm.

"It's his arm," Maria said. Ferdinand was too much in shock still to say anything. I have to admit that so was I—for different reasons.

"Let me take him back and take a look at it," Prentice said. A half hour later, he came back out. "I've done what I can, but it's a bad break. He needs to go to the hospital. And he's in shock. They'll need to keep him for observation of that. I've put a splint on it until he can get to the hospital."

"Thank you, doctor. We'll take him home," Maria said, her jaw set.

"He needs to go to the hospital," Prentice said.

"He can't afford to go to the hospital," she stubbornly responded.

For the first time Prentice looked at me fully, and it was the first time I was able to look fully back at him.

"Tell me which hospital to go to, and if you'll call them to expect him, I'll take him there . . . and pay for the treatment," I said in a low voice. I was already touting up in my mind how many sailors that would be, but what the hell? It was just sex.

Prentice gave me a long look. "I'll do better than that," he said. "I'll go with you and talk to the doctors there in person. And I'll share the cost with you."

After Ferdinand had been carted up to a ward at the hospital, Prentice turned to me and said, "That was a generous thing you did for that man. I'm Paul Prentice, by the way."

"I know who you are," I answered. "I'm Keith Evans."

"I know who you are too," he said and smiled at me. I smiled back. He reached out and touched my forearm and I knew then that we would fuck.

"I appreciate what you did as much as Ferdinand will, Keith. I run a free clinic to help as many as I can, but sometimes more needs to be done than I can do. When that's the case, it breaks my heart. Perhaps you'll join me in a drink this evening so I can show my appreciation."

"Yes, I guess I can do that," I said. Yep, I knew we were going to fuck. He knew it too.

"Say the Surfer's Point Bar at the Sheraton Laguna at 6:30? I'll have to stay to closing at the clinic."

"Yes, that's fine," I answered. "6:30." We weren't going to fuck at his house then—or, at least, we weren't going to have the obligatory preliminary drink and waltz around each other at his house.

He turned to leave but then turned back. "Are you going to break my heart, Keith?"

Yep, we definitely were going to fuck. "I don't know," I answered. "We'll have to see."

"You know what I want," he said.

"Yes, I know what you want."

We had two drinks at the Surfer's Point Bar and a bit of conversation. Prentice was an Australian, on

33

Guam because after doing his internship in the poorer areas of Sydney, he wanted to go the free clinic route. The job had opened up here and he'd been here for fifteen years.

"And what brought you to Guam, Keith? You're not from here are you?"

"No, I'm from the States—South Carolina. A southern boy. I heard the surf was great here and I'd read about Gauguin and his retreat to Tahiti to paint in peace. I also heard that living was cheap here—and, all cards on the table, I heard that sailors took shore leave here."

I looked at him to see if this would make him get up and leave, but he didn't, so I continued. "I guess Guam is the poor boy's Tahiti. And I was a poor boy when I came here. I'm basically a free spirit, I think. My father has often said I'm a hippie born too late."

"Are you still a poor boy, Keith?"

"I make do. I sell some paintings. I intend to sell more." I'd dropped the hint, but I didn't want to say straight out that it was the paid sex that sustained me here. He probably knew I was a rent-boy, but I didn't want that to be between us from the beginning—the beginning of what I didn't want to think about.

But then he obviated the need to think about it. He placed a hand on my forearm and said, "I've taken the liberty of booking a room upstairs in the hotel. Will you go upstairs with me?"

I looked into his searching eyes. "Yes, you already knew I would."

"I'm versatile, but—"

"So am I. I usually bottom, though."

He smiled. "I should warn you. You are a small young man. I'm built big."

"I've done all sizes."

"Built big" was an understatement. He wasn't as long as Lee Houser was, but close. He had to be ten inches hard. But where Houser was thin, Prentice was thick, and that more than made up for the difference. And he was virile. He could shoot, recharge, and score again within the span of fifteen minutes.

We held there on the bed in the hotel room, each of us, I know, counting the ejaculations, as he pumped cum again and again into the bulb of the condom deep inside me. I was arched back on the bed, my weight on my shoulder blades, my legs running up his muscular chest, and him kneeling between my legs, holding my buttocks up with his strong hands. He was buried ten inches inside me.

One, two, three . . . four my mind screamed as I counted each clutching of his buttocks, jerk, and huff as he pumped cum inside me.

He let my hips down easy, pulling only a couple of inches back, leaned his face down to mine, and we went into a deep kiss.

"That was nice, very nice. I've been wanting to do that to you since I saw you at the bar in Denial," he said when we'd come out of the kiss. Although going mostly flaccid, he was gently moving his cock in and out of me, still deep. keeping us both aware he was still inside me.

His hands went to my hair, which was down, and he ran his fingers through the strands, straightening out the knots.

"Yes, that was nice," I responded. "If I knew you were that big, though, I would have been scared."

"That's why I didn't pursue you at Denial. You looked too small to take me."

"What changed your mind?" I asked.

"When I saw you in the fashion show I knew you could take it."

"How did that tell you so?"

"You were modeling for Lee Houser. Lee fucks all of his models. He's fucked you, hasn't he?"

"Yes." I saw no reason to deny it.

"I know how long Lee is. I knew you could take me then."

"You're a lot thicker than Houser is," I said.

"And you took it, didn't you?"

"Barely."

"Enough. Yes, enough. You're big too, especially for the size of your body."

"And you want—?"

"Yes, it's my turn." He rolled off me and then, crowned me with a condom, and climbed back on top of me, positioning my cock at his hole and slowly, breathing hard and letting his breath out in puffs, descended on my cock. I held onto his waist—thick but manly, his abs sculpted like the armor of a Roman soldier—as he rode my cock. His dick bounced up and down on my stomach, until I grasped it and stroked it as he rode me to my ejaculation—not as dramatic or copious as his was. When I'd come, he leaned his face down to mine and we kissed deeply again.

"You don't mind that I'm a . . ." I couldn't finish that.

"Yes, I mind very much. I want you all to myself." He said it in a joking manner, but I later realized I should have taken it more seriously. "But right now, I want to possess you again—make you all mine, if just for now."

"A request," I said.

"What?"

"Could you open the windows? I'd like to be able to hear the surf from the ocean. Maybe you could try to match the rhythm of the sound of the surf with your thrusts?"

He laughed, bounding off the bed to open the windows. And then, putting me on my knees, cheek to pillow, he mounted my hips, invaded me deep, and slow pumped me to the rhythm of the surf. Even his spasm of release matched the rhythm of the surf.

"I want you to come back to the clinic with me," he whispered in my ear as we lay there, me in his embrace, both listening to the sound of the surf, both fondling the cock of the other.

"When? Why?"

"Now."

"The clinic will be closed."

"Not to me. I'm the senior doctor there."

"Why?"

"I want to give you an HIV test."

"I had one four days ago—at your clinic. But why anyway? We used rubbers."

"How many men have fucked you since you had that test?"

"Three. No, four. You've fucked me too and I haven't asked you to test."

"I do test. I will test tonight too. I want you to take the test because I have to have you bareback. I want it to be natural with you. I can do the test. It won't take long."

We both tested negative—according to him.

He fucked me on an exam table, with my legs spread and raised and my feet in stirrups. My arms were pulled down the side of the table and restrained there.

He told me that binding his partner heightened his arousal. I admitted that being bound heightened mine as well. I was completely at his mercy. He took advantage of that, taking me hard and rough. I loved it.

He wore an open white lab coat for effect—and nothing else. I was naked. He stood between my spread thighs, ran his long, thick cock up into my ass, and leaned over me, his hands pressed into my pecs, his thumbs thrumbing my nipples, his eyes locked on mine as he fucked, fucked, fucked me in long, deep slides, raw, throbbing cock flesh stretching undulating passage walls and, one squirt, two squirts, three and four squirts seeded me deep inside. I writhed under him as much as my bindings permitted, crying out my passion and the totality of being taken to the walls of the deserted clinic. I went totally quiet though and passive as I felt him tense and counted in a shaky voice the number of times he jerked and released: one, two, three, four.

I had been royally fucked and bred, flesh rubbing directly on flesh.

* * * *

We slept, him on top of me on a bed off the staff break room at the clinic, rousing an hour before dawn to be out of the clinic before the staff started to arrive and it opened. There wasn't much sleep to be had. He couldn't get enough cum into me, fucking me for fifteen minutes of every forty-five. If I were a woman I'd be having sextuplets in another nine months. He reveled in the barebacking. So did I.

"You've told me you go surfing at dawn," he whispered.

"Is that what you want to do? To watch me surfing at dawn?" I asked.

"Yes, now, please."

I took him to my beach, making him go down to the beach while I retrieved my board and towels from my shack. He sat on a towel on the beach, just in his briefs, as I surfed the sun up over the ocean. When I came out of the water and walked toward him, I saw that he had his briefs off and was in massive erection again. I took him to a secluded place on the beach where a sandy patch was surrounded by rocks near the face of the cliff above the beach. He fucked me there again. He went down on the towel cross-legged, and I sat in his lap, on his cock, facing him, my ankles hooked behind him above the curve of his buttocks, and we embraced each other and just rocked back and forth, our rocking motion moving his unsheathed cock inside me until his warm semen flowed deep in my core once more.

"You found a surfboard somewhere," he whispered. "Do you live near here?"

"Yes, just at the top of the beach," I said. "Do you want me to show it to you?" I'd never brought a man home to my shack—certainly not a man who was fucking me. I'd kept my rent-boy activities entirely separate from my private life.

"Are there examples of your artwork there?"

"Yes, it's my studio too."

It took him no time at all to find the painting I'd done of him—imagined—in the nude. I, of course, hadn't done his genitals anything close to justice.

"It's of me," he said, his voice full of awe, as he stood in front of the painting.

"Yes, I'll have to fix that," I said, pointing to the cock in the painting.

"You know what that makes me want to do, don't you?" he said.

"I'm sore. I bet you are too. And don't you have to go to work? Aren't there patients at the clinic who need you to go to work today?"

"Tonight then. Come to the clinic at 6:30 and we'll go someplace."

The someplace was a room at the Sheraton Laguna again. The next day's someplace was here, at my shack. The someplaces from then always were somewhere other than where he lived. After a week, it had become just the clinic after hours and my shack. We were, of course, still barebacking, and that was nice. But I was getting itchy, without really understanding why.

When he popped the proposal, I understood why.

"I don't want you to have to be a rent-boy anymore," he said.

"I'm not a rent-boy because I have to be," I said. "I am a male whore because I choose to be. It frees me to be what I want to be."

"I want you to be mine—exclusively," he said. "Don't you like the barebacking? If it's just me, we can bareback to our heart's content. We don't have to take the tests all the time."

"Yes, the barebacking is nice, but—" I didn't fill in what the "but" was, but it struck me that the "but" was that it took variety from me and it put me in the control of one man. I would become Paul's mistress—exclusively Paul's. Just another of Paul's possessions.

"I want you to be—I don't know what they call a man who is one—I want you to be my mistress. Exclusively mine. I'd pay all your bills. You could paint and surf to your heart's content and you wouldn't have to open your legs for any other man."

"It's something to consider," I said, knowing that, in fact, it wasn't.

When he left, I found a wad of bills on the counter beside my painting of him. $500. I hadn't asked him for money the entire time we'd been together. Somehow it cheapened what we had together. It was no different from taking money from anyone else fucking me, of course, but it put Paul in the same league—buying my time. Buying me, my body. Making me just an object of his obsession.

I got a call from Lee Houser the next day. "I'd like you to come over—to spend the night. I have someone here who I'm trying to make a deal with. I think you'd like him. I'll pay you well, of course."

I went. The friend was black and big, a bull of a man. I don't know what the deal was other than that it included me from Houser's side. The black bull fucked me on a bed in the guest room for an hour, snorting like the bull he was and pounding away inside me with a big black cock, giving me no quarter, slapping me around when I struggled with him. It was exactly what I needed, what I'd missed after a week of Paul.

Afterward Houser took me to his bed and gave me a foot of cock. That job was gloriously welcome. They'd both barebacked me. I no longer was exclusively Paul's on the strength of the last HIV test he'd given me. I was what I was in Guam to be—a rent-boy.

When I left the house there was a big black limousine parked beside my Jeep. As I came around to the driver's side of my Wrangler, the back passenger side window of the limo slid down and the black man who had fucked me earlier in the day showed his face.

"I like to think I haven't finished with you, young man," he said. "Come into the car and drive to my hotel with me. I'll take you to dinner there and then I'll pay you $1,000 for the use of your body through the night."

The use of my body. No "make love to you." Not even "fuck you." I don't know why, but that sounded so real to me, so expressive of the impersonal nature of the business I sought—not intruding on my surfing or painting even a bit.

"I have my car here," I said, shrugging my shoulders.

"And is that the only reason you won't go with me?"

I thought about that. Turning him down hadn't been my first reaction. That was somewhat of a revelation. Until then I'd assumed that I'd be taking Paul Prentice up on his offer of a more permanent, exclusive relationship. But I hadn't hesitated in accepting Lee Houser's summons to come entertain someone he had a business deal with. I'd known what that entertainment would entail. I also had known that, once at Houser's house, I'd let him fuck me again too with that snake of his—if he wanted me. And I would have been disappointed if he hadn't wanted me. I'd been disappointed that he had chosen that Tyler kid last time as well as me. I realized I looked forward to a foot of Houser's snake inside me.

"Yes," I said. "That's the only reason I couldn't come."

"The price is right and the service expected acceptable?"

"Yes, there's just the logistics involved."

"I have an extra man in front here. Would you let him drive your car to the hotel? He'd pay for valet parking for it. I'm at the Dusit Thani Resort."

Ah, five stars and on the ocean, I thought. But I'm not sure my old Wrangler would be acceptable there.

"Can you hear the surf of the ocean from your room?" I asked.

"Excuse me?"

"Never mind. A private joke."

"Yes, I can hear the sound of the ocean from my suite," he said. "Does that help you to decide to accept my offer?"

He wanted me. He wanted me enough to essentially plead with me to come to him. I wondered, though, why I couldn't just drive my own car there. I didn't ask, and it's just as well that I didn't. He wanted me in the limo because he wanted to start using my body immediately.

The driver took the long route to the hotel, because the man buying my body—after telling me his name was Kwame and he was from Nigeria—pulled me onto his lap, had my trousers off while he was pawing me and his own fly open, and had me bouncing on his thick cock, yodeling, and bareback seeded once again before we reached the hotel. The driver had taken twenty minutes for a ten-minute drive. Kwame took his time fucking a man.

He fed me at the hotel's Aqua buffet restaurant, winking at me and telling me to eat hearty to keep my strength up. Once in his room, which indeed was an ocean-front suite, and where, indeed, I could hear the sound of the surf crashing on the beach, he held me in the bed for eight hours, fucking me with his big black bull cock for a half hour every two hours. He didn't just want to fuck me. He wanted me to resist until overpowered, which he easily could do. And he wanted to slap me around. And he wanted to bind my wrists together with leather cords and take it from me. For $1,000 I let him do what he wanted. And most of the time I enjoyed the intensity and variety of it—and that big black cock that nearly dislocated my jaw when he made me take it in my mouth.

Yes, I could be in the big time if I let Houser set up trysts like this.

When I finally was able to get off the bed to go to the shower, I squished inside while I staggered from all the Nigerian cum inside me. He fucked me in the shower too.

He paid me the $1,000 and threw in a 100-dollar tip. I called Lee Houser to report on the encounter and to hope it helped him with his deal.

"I'm glad you went with him," Houser said. "Yes, you've helped me with my deal." He still didn't tell me what the deal had been and I surmised I really didn't want to know. The Nigerian looked like a thug and he fucked like a thug. I certainly had been well and cruelly fucked—I'd even say ravished. "That can be the first of many such lucrative arrangements for you," Houser went on to say. "You won't have to work the streets anymore if you let me take care of you."

I disconnected with that phrase in my mind—"if you let me take care of you." Suddenly there were two men who wanted to own me. Is that what I came to Guam to do? Is that what being an out-of-period hippie was all about?

One thing I knew I'd have to do. The next time Paul Prentice came sniffing around me I'd have to tell him that he wasn't the last man who had barebacked me, bred me, and filled me to overflowing with his cum.

* * * *

Paul hadn't missed me. He'd had to make an emergency trip to the States with a patient. He came to my shack for a nooner two days after I'd been bareback laid by Houser and the Nigerian thug. I had to tell him that we'd have to use a condom until he checked me again unless he wanted to take the risk.

"You what? We're supposed to be exclusive," he said, exploding.

"I haven't promised to be exclusive yet," I answered. "And you know Lee Houser. He thinks he owns me." I came close to pointing out that Paul thought he owned me too and didn't have a bill of sale on me any more than Lee Houser had. I had not meant for this rent-boy business to be this complicated. I'd thought it would be pretty straightforward. I didn't see it as having these pitfalls.

Paul still wanted to lay me, and groused, but accepted that we'd use a condom, which we did. He fucked me on my bed, which is only a three-quarters, taking me in a side split. Although I could feel him tense and jerk several times, with the condom I couldn't be precise enough with the blasts of cum to count them.

We lay there, me in his embrace, him still inside me, and, starting with noticing a water spot in the ceiling, he started ticking off improvements he'd pay for to make this a neat little love nest for us.

"It's not the same now that we've barebacked," he groused, no longer talking about the deficiencies of my place.

"No, it's not," I admitted.

Out of the blue then, not really having been thinking about it, although it must have been there in my subconscious all along, I blurted out, "If this place doesn't meet your specifications, why don't we fuck at your place, Paul? You haven't taken me to your place yet."

He froze. I could feel his body tense up and he took air in and seemed to take the longest time to exhale it again. "My neighborhood isn't the best place to be conducting this sort of activity."

"What's wrong with this sort of activity between two willing men?" I asked. "It's not like you're married or anything."

I could feel him tense again. But I also could feel him hardening up again. He took being in heat again as an escape from talking to me about where we fucked. "I don't have long before I have to go back and you have me hard again. Roll over on your belly and go up on your knees."

I did so, he changed condoms, and I let him mount my ass and fuck me again. I didn't bring up the question of fucking at his place again—then or even later.

When he left, he said, "Come by the clinic at 6:30. We'll do the tests again."

"I'm sorry, I can't tonight, Paul, I have an appointment tonight to show some of my painting to a potential buyer—a woman," I said, not knowing then why I said that. I didn't have any appointment that night. I just didn't want to go to the clinic and put myself under Paul's control again by having an HIV test run. He never showed me the result of his own tests. I couldn't even be sure he actually ran the tests on himself.

"Then tomorrow night," he said. "I don't want to go long without being able to bareback you."

After he left and I thought about it, I knew why I was going to be busy that night. I borrowed the car Sid Tanner, the guy in the wheel chair—whose cock I continued to ride because there was no way he was contracting HIV as isolated and alone as he was— owned so that others could run errands for him, and at 6:30 I was parked up the street from Paul's clinic. I followed him through the town to a very nice residential neighborhood, where a garage door lifted when he turned his BMW into the driveway. There was a late-model SUV in the garage as well. He came out of the garage and tossed a ball between two teenage boys in the front yard for a minute or two, and when he went to the front door, he was greeting with a kiss from a woman.

I drove from there to Denial, tossed back two drinks, picked out the meanest looking sailor who was sniffing around me, showed him where the Ypao Breeze Inn was, and let him bang the hell out of me for $30 plus the cost of the room. I let him bareback me. He enjoyed it and obviously considered himself lucky. I enjoyed it too, as it was completely my own decision, my own risk.

I didn't give a shit what Paul would think about it.

I didn't go to the clinic at 6:30 the next night. I didn't answer Paul's telephone call at 7:00. And I turned the lights off in the shack and just sat staring at the painting of him—which I had meanwhile altered to be anatomically correct. Where I'd placed it, the moonlight through the window wall lit it up. When he came and banged on the door at 7:30, I sat quiet as a mouse and didn't answer the door.

The next day I wrapped the painting of him up and had a delivery service take it to his house. I'd noted the address down when I followed him there. It was 50-50 whether or not he'd be the one to receive the package at the house. I thought those odds were fair.

I racked my brain to think whether or not I'd ever asked him if he was married before—to a woman—and had children at home he was a father to. If he'd told me, I wouldn't have gotten involved with him. My father had left my mother and run off with a man. That had left scars—and it probably had helped send me in the direction to going with men. But he'd been honest enough to break off his relationship with a family. He hadn't tried to have it all. And he hadn't, like Paul had, expected his male lover to be fully dedicated to the relationship.

In ensuing weeks, I'd rethought this and decided I'd been hasty—that the wife and children didn't deserve finding out this way, if at all. But then, if Paul did it with me, I bet he'd done it with others.

He did try to call and to come to the shack a couple of times in the next week. But I avoided him.

He even came down to the beach at dawn one morning and sat on a towel watching me surf. But I stayed out in the ocean until he had left.

Then it stopped, and I was sure he'd found some other free spirit to break.

* * * *

"Keith? Lee Houser here. I have a Korean businessman here who I've told about you. I sent you a DVD he did for you to look at. Did you receive it?"

"Yes," I answered. "I'm looking at it now." And I *was* looking at it. The Korean was tall and slim and wiry. He was quite athletic too, wearing only a leather harness on his chest, black boots, and black leather wristbands. I found him sexy. I wouldn't mind being dominated by him. The film had been going on for twenty minutes before Houser called me. The Korean was seriously hung—almost as much as Houser was from the look of it. The film had started with a shot of a naked and impressively erect late-thirtyish Korean, holding a whip, forcing a small, naked blond youth to his knees in front of him with a cruel grip of his head hair, forcing the huge cock between the youth's lips, and side-arm whipping the blond's buttocks. The strength of the lash was more dramatic than painful, but the young man flinched with each blow—not, however, enough to dislodge the Korean's cock from his throat. The film was giving the impression of suggestive arousal more than actual brutality—at least that's what I took from it, already in the grip of the dominating Korean.

"Do you like what you see?" Houser asked over the telephone connection.

"Do you mean am I beating off to it?"

"That would be an indication, yes," he said, laughing.

"Yes," I admitted. It had made me go hard; it had made me stroke myself. "I'm afraid so," I added, aware of the danger of enjoying what I saw and imagining it was happening to me.

This scene moved into a sequence shot from across the table of the small, blond guy—maybe eighteen or nineteen, not more than a year younger than I was—belly down on the top of a table, his face pointed at the camera. He was clutching the table top on either side of him at the edge. There was no doubt from his facial expression that he was being fucked hard and deep. The Korean was saddled up behind him, holding the young man's hips between his hands. The Korean had a blissful, satisfied look on his face. The camera panned around to the side of the tableau, providing a shot of the long, thin cock taking long strokes into the blond's ass. The Korean reached up, grabbed a hank of the youth's blond curls and arched the young man's torso back cruelly. The youth cried out, "Oh, shit, oh, fuck!"

The young man screamed this same phrase at intervals throughout the video—providing a notion of a limited vocabulary of being taken on his part and a similarity between this film and most other porn vids.

In the next shot, the young man was suspended over the carpet, his arms stretched out in front of him, grasping the edge of the table. His body streamed back to the Korean's. The Korean was standing in a crouch between the young man's thighs, his hands holding the blond's body up by clutching his waist, and the hands pulling the youth's buttocks back and forth on the

Korean's cock. This transitioned into the Korean lying on his back on the table with the blond youth suspended over his body in a crab position, the youth's hands and feet flat on the table on either side of the Korean's body and his pelvis rising and falling on the Korean's cock. The Korean transitioned from this to grabbing the young man under his knees and raising and spreading his legs. Somehow the Korean had gotten his chin under the youth's chin and forced the young blond's head to arch back severely. The Korean was fucking up into the young man's hole, and the youth was gurgling, his face showing the intensity of the taking to the camera.

"Kim has watched the film you did the day of the fashion show, Keith," Houser said over the phone. "He's making a week-long trip to Honolulu and would like some companionship. He's good, very, very good. I know this for a fact. He's hung like an elephant."

"Yes, I can see that," I answered.

"You can see for yourself that he'll give you a good fuck. He'll pay you $5,000 and cover all expenses if you'll go to Honolulu and let him use you when and as he likes. What do you have to say about that?"

I zipped the DVD back and started watching it from the beginning again. "Sorry, Lee, but I meant to tell you sooner. I've given up that business. My paintings are selling well now, and I've signed up for a surfboard contest and have to do a lot of practicing. Best of luck in finding someone for this Korean dude. He's seriously hung, yes he is."

I only half listened to his arguments and he eventually got the idea and let me go.

I felt a great burden lifting off my shoulders. I felt free.

The telephone rang again.

"Yes, I do that," I said in answer to the question from the sailor saying he was just off the ship on shore leave and had been given my card. "Do you have a photo to show me?"

"OK, good." Better than good if it really was him. It was a naked shot. He was built and good looking—and young. Older than I was but still in his twenties.

"Here's my photo. And another one. Still interested?"

"OK, good. I'll let you do just about anything you want as often as you want all night for $100 plus the hotel. There's one near where you're calling from called the Ypao Breeze Inn that asks no questions and charges $50 a night. Anything you want, although I have some suggestions you might be interested in. If you want it, book the room and call me back to give me the room number. Have the money on the desk for me to see when I enter the room."

* * * *

I was belly down on the bed, feet on the floor, facing a mirror on the opposite wall. My arms were raised over my head, gripping the edge of the mattress on the other side. The hunky young, muscular sailor was saddled up behind me, grabbing my hips between his hands and rapidly pulling me on and off his thick cock, banging the hell out of me. We were both looking into the mirror, at each other, our faces showing the lust and pleasure we were getting. Two young, healthy bodies banging away at each other. He came in a gush of cum, filling the bulb of his rubber. He pulled the rubber off his cock and threw it on the floor.

Forty minutes later, I was gripping the edge of the desk in the Ypao Breeze Inn room, with my body suspended straight out behind me, my legs streaming around the sailor's slim hips and tight ass. He was crouched a bit between my legs, holding my waist between his hands, and pulling me on and off his cock. Banging the hell out of me again. He was young, virile, and ready to go again constantly. He tensed and jerked, I cried out, "Oh, shit. Oh, fuck," and he came in a gush of cum, filling the bulb of his rubber. I heard the snap of the rubber being pulled off and turned my head to see him toss it, thick as a sea slug with cum, on the floor.

I ached that it be barebacking, but I couldn't chance it.

Forty-five minutes later the sailor was on his back on the bed, and I was suspended above him in a crab position, my hands and feet flat on the mattress on either side of his body. He held my waist between his hands and I raised and lowered my pelvis, taking his cock deep inside my passage. He tensed, pushed me off to the side on my back, went up on his knees, jerked the rubber off his cock and came on my chest and belly. The used rubber was flipped to the floor.

Twenty minutes later I was lying on the foot of the bed, my thighs spread, my legs dangling toward the floor. The hunky young sailor was kneeling on the floor between my thighs, working my anal hole with his mouth and fingers. I was pulling on my cock. I tensed, jerked, and shot my load toward the ceiling in a high arc of cum. The sailor stood, crowned himself with a rubber, grabbed my ankles with his hands, cruelly

53

wishboned my legs, moved in with his erection, skewered me, and started banging the hell out of me again. "Oh, shit. Oh, fuck!" I cried out.

An hour later, he came back from having a smoke at the window. I was lying on my side on the bed, panting lightly and staring at the door into the bathroom of the small, tawdry room. I had told him he could go all night if he wanted to for the $150, but I hadn't imagined that he would. I heard the snap of the rubber being pulled into place. There were four—or maybe five, I'd lost count—spent ones on the floor. He was young, virile, full of cum, and perpetually hard. He grabbed my ankles and pulled my legs down to where my butt came to the edge of the foot of the bed. I moaned and half turned to my back, but he bent and pushed my upward leg up into my chest, moving me back to my side. I felt the bulb of the cock at my now-gaping hole as he gave me three inches.

"Oh, shit. Oh, fuck," I murmured in an exhausted voice, and holding the ankle of the bent leg in one hand and grasping my other thigh with the other, he pushed his hard cock up into my passage, compressed now by the position of my thighs, giving him a tighter channel than he'd had since the first reaming, and started a slow, rhythmic fuck. I raised my arm, pressing my hand into the cleft between his pecs, grabbing hold of a set of dog tags he had nestled there, hanging on a chain. I wasn't trying to push him away; I was too tired to do that. It was more to feel him there, working me, to make more of a connection between us than his dick inside me and his hands on my thighs. But, to tell the truth, having the dick of a virile, young, handsome sailor inside me was all right too. I moaned. "Oh, shit. Oh, fuck."

"I've got one night of shore leave," he murmured. "Got a whole lot of cum to dump. Guess it's your lucky night, blondie."

I was just a sailor's cheap one-night shore leave rent-boy lay on the remote dumpy rock of an island, Guam, again. But I made all of my own decisions for what I was going to let a man do to me and I was a free spirit.

When the sun came up, I was alone in the room at last, lying on my side, my knees curled up into my stomach, moaning and still panting. The sailor hadn't left more than fifteen minutes before. I knew my hole was gaping and rubbed raw, my passage pulsating. He'd fucked me through the night, getting the most bang he could for his $150. One of Lee Houser's clients would have paid me that much just to suck him off once. But I felt strangely satisfied.

~

Aloha Week

Tyler Sinclair arched his head back on the bed in the somewhat seedy Ypao Breeze Inn room on Guam's western Tumon tourist coast and moaned deeply. The sailor was in deep and was slow pumping him. He'd been slow pumping him for an eternity, edging him, holding off on his ejaculation. Tyler had already come, taking care of himself with his own hand. But the Sailor wanted the biggest bang for his buck. Whenever he reached the edge, he stopped and held them there, Tyler's pelvis being arched up to the big sailor's pelvis, the young whore's legs spread and bent, his feet pressed into the edge of the foot of the bed.

Tyler's cell phone was on the nightstand. He could see it now that his head was arched back. It was vibrating. A call was coming in. He could feel the sailor tensing, ready to blow, but also ready to edge himself again. Tyler put his hips into motion in the crucial seconds, going up on his elbows, thrusting his hips forward as the sailor thrust his cock forward. He called out, "Fuck, yes, you beautiful black brute. Let me have your cum. Blast me with your fuckin' big cock. Show me what you got. Make me feel it!"

Jolted by the sudden stroking of his manhood, the sailor went over the edge. In three jerks he filled the bulb of his condom, pulled out of Tyler's ass, and, after giving Tyler a slap on his butt, had risen from the bed and was padding off to the bathroom.

When he heard the shower start, Tyler rolled off the bed, went around to the nightstand, and pushed some buttons on the cell phone.

"Did you call me just now, Mr. Houser?" Lee Houser was someone important who lived in a mansion hanging off a cliff on the coast north of Tumon. He did a lot of things, including running a stable of high-priced male whores. Tyler wasn't in that stable, but he'd like to be. Houser rented out to the wealthier class of johns on the island, mostly businessmen here permanently. Tyler serviced cash-strapped horny sailors on shore leave at the naval base to the south. He depended on word-of-mouth references.

Tyler had recently spent a night in Houser's bed with another sub after substituting as a model in a charity men's fashion show Houser had held in his house. The mixed American-Japanese man had fucked Tyler four times in the night—with the longest cock Tyler had ever taken. It must have been nearly a foot long hard. It was thin, but hard, and it had gone right into the quick of Tyler. Every time, it had conquered him, sliding in slowly to the quick as he held there docile, panting lightly, gasping, concentrating on how far up into his gut it was. Then Tyler felt himself emitting the long sigh as it was slowly withdrawn nearly the whole way. He would clutch at the man's buttocks then, feeling the loss of the cock. And he then would lie back docilely, gasping as it glided in deep again. And again and again, Tyler surrendering completely to the man's long cock a long time before the man flooding him deep with cum.

Houser had barebacked him. Tyler had had to be tested right before doing the fashion show. Houser wasn't the only one who fucked him that day. The models had been auctioned off to the men who'd come to the show—and Tyler had been put in a taxing porn vid too.

Houser had complimented Tyler on how he had performed. Tyler hoped that would pan out to some gigs with high payers. And here the man was, on the cell phone.

"Can you break away for a week?" Houser asked over the phone. "There's a Korean businessman here who is going to Honolulu for a week and who wants a companion. It would be $5,000 for you to give him whatever he wants as often as he wants while you're with him—plus all expenses. Plane fare, hotel, meals and all. You'd have to take an HIV test tomorrow. He barebacks, he's demanding, and he's seriously hung. I can't say you won't be fully earning the five thou. You'd be doing me a big favor, that I'd be returning if you do good. You'd need to be at the airport at 9:00 p.m. It's a night flight."

Tyler was sitting on the side of the bed, facing the bathroom door, when he set the cell phone back down on the nightstand. The sailor padded out of the bathroom, holding a towel around his waist. He let it drop to reveal that he was in erection again. He wasn't the most handsome sailor Tyler had serviced but he was built. He was on the short side—as was Tyler— and was stocky, but he was muscular and didn't have much fat on him. He had a cock and balls to be proud of. He was the proverbial black bull. Black curls swirled all over his body, with a trail coming down from his hair-covered pecs into his trimmed bush. He shrugged at Tyler in a "What can you do?" silent expression of half apology for what he then was going to do.

"What can I say?" he asked. "I've been at sea for a while and I'm horny as hell."

He paid for multiples, so there wasn't much else to say, so Tyler simply said, "Let's see what we can do about your problem, sailor."

He came to Tyler and stood there in front of the young whore, while Tyler, grasping the sailor's hips in his hands, took the cock in his mouth and sucked it to throbbing and the sailor to shuddering and groaning.

Not being able to take any more, the sailor reached down and grasped Tyler's ankles and dragged the small rent-boy back across the bed to the foot, where he put Tyler down on his belly, with his feet on the floor. Tyler saw, out of the corner of his eye, the sailor reach down and pull the black belt out of his white trousers, which were puddled on the floor at the foot of the bed. Breathing heavy, heavy with need, he roughly grabbed Tyler's wrists, tied them together behind his back with the belt, put himself in position behind the young man's ass, snapped a condom on, saddled up, and penetrated Tyler's passage with his cock. He slid right in, having reamed the whore to his specs earlier.

"Oh, shit, Oh, fuck, you're big," Tyler cried out. "You're a fuckin' black bull." He knew the sailor wanted to hear something like that, but he was pretty big. And he was young, muscular, and virile. It's why Tyler went with sailors. It wasn't just for the money—which wasn't much, with sailors—it was because they mostly were young, virile, muscular, and came in from the sea randy, their eyeballs swimming in unreleased cum. They came in from the ocean with only one thing in mind—getting laid—and they were usually easily controlled as long as you waved your hole at them and surrendered to their needs—or at least could convince them you had.

"But you'll take it, won't you?" he growled. "So sweet. With your size and those slim hips, I didn't know if you could take it. But you open right up for me, don't you, baby? Ahhh, that's nice." He grabbed Tyler's hips and started pounding away. As he got close, the young whore knew he'd edge off—that he'd do that as often as he could before he shot off. And there wasn't much Tyler could do about that in this position. He was completely at the sailor's mercy.

Tyler relaxed his channel, willing the muscles of his passage walls to milk the dick churning inside it, and enjoyed the fuck, thinking thoughts of the beaches of Hawaii. Surely an older Korean businessman couldn't take him any harder than this—and he'd pay a whole hell of a lot more than this black boy was paying.

* * * *

Tyler met Song Rhee for the first time in the airport departure lounge. He was tall, wiry, and not bad looking. He was maybe in his early forties. There was a look of mystery and danger about him but he walked and talked like a man in control. Although he acknowledged the young rent-boy was there, his attention until they got on the plane, in side-by-side first-class seats, him on the aisle and Tyler at the window, was taken up with business calls. He spoke in Korean on the phone, but it was clear that he was giving, not receiving, instructions and orders.

They engaged in neutral chit chat during the snack service, the Korean asking the personal questions, not revealing anything about himself, and not saying much. He spoke impeccable English, but you could tell that it wasn't his native language.

"I'm from San Diego," Tyler answered to one question and, "I came out here with a Naval officer. He went to his next assignment without me," Tyler responded to the follow-up question. He didn't elaborate on how he'd been a beach bum, riding the surf board, not going back East with his parents when they'd left San Diego, with the excuse that he wanted to finish the junior college course he'd started. He couldn't tell them that he didn't want to leave the boyfriend who was fucking him. The boyfriend left; the fucking didn't, and in short order he was doing it for money. Dirk, the Naval officer, had said he was in love with Tyler and wanted Tyler to go to Guam with him—where, he said, the surf was good for boarding. Tyler believed him and found himself in Guam, where Tyler found that the only thing the Navy guy hadn't lied about was that the surf on Guam was good for boarding. After a year, Tyler had been left high and dry—and in need of money. Thus, the sailors. End of the longer version of the story that he didn't tell the Korean. Rhee didn't seem to mind.

"I'm twenty-one," Tyler said to another question. "Yes, I know I don't look it. Do you mind?"

The Korean said he didn't mind, but he didn't take the conversation any farther in that direction during the snack service.

"I've had two years of community college—in San Diego," Tyler answered to yet another question. "I didn't specialize in anything really. What I like to do is go out in the surf on my board."

The snack service over, the lights were dimmed in the cabin. It was a night flight.

The Korean turned in his seat toward Tyler. He placed a hand on Tyler's cheek and ran his fingers into Tyler's shoulder-length blond hair. He grasped the hair hard and pulled Tyler's head back painfully. The young man wanted to yelp, but he didn't. There was a cruel leer on the Korean's face, but it lasted but a moment— enough to put Tyler off center—before the Korean's smile mellowed and he loosened his grip on Tyler's hair. Rhee leaned in for a kiss and Tyler opened his lips to the man, being surprised that the Korean, so formal, stiff, and distant before now, gave him tongue.

It wasn't a long kiss, not something that anyone walking the aisle was likely to notice. But no one was walking the aisle. First class wasn't full and the stewardesses were busy putting the snack service away and were settling in for some quiet time themselves.

"I'm a little worried," the Korean said when they came out of the kiss. "You are smaller than I thought you'd be. Your hips are slim, you're very womanish, you know. I'm not complaining about that. You are a beautiful young man. But your hips are so slim. Lee Houser told me that he has had you. True?"

"Yes," Tyler answered.

"I know he is impressively long. Did you . . . ?"

"Yes, I managed him."

"All of it?"

"Yes. Not easily, of course. But not easily is good, isn't it? If it's difficult for you, don't they feel more satisfied?"

"Yes, very good." That cruel leer passed over the Korean's face again, but then it was gone. "He isn't terribly thick though, I believe."

"No. But terribly long."

"I'm thick too," the Korean stated, but then he went right on. He'd put his left arm around Tyler's neck and had his right hand on Tyler's right thigh. He used that to tease Tyler's thighs to spread. Then he had his hand on Tyler's basket.

"I want you to control yourself," he said in a low voice. "I'm going to explore you and you will orgasm for me. But I want you to remain quiet. Do you understand?"

"Yes," Tyler answered. He both heard the sound of his zipper being pulled down and felt the release of the pressure he'd felt down there, as he had been hardening up.

"Do you want me to unzip you too?" he asked.

"Yes," the Korean answered.

Tyler did so and they both released and fisted each other's cocks. It was dark in the confines of their seats, and Rhee's body was turned toward the window. You would have had to lean into the seat to see what the two were doing, and the section was settled down for the night.

"You are a beautiful young man," Rhee said. "Almost as much woman as man during sex, I imagine, but you have a very nice cock. Very slim hips." The man seemed to be obsessed with whether Tyler had a hole that would take him and seemed to believe that the slimness of hips had something to do with that. Tyler wasn't sure if the man would be displeased if he did have trouble taking the cock. And what a cock it was, Tyler was finding by feeling it up. He was finding that Rhee's cock was way beyond nice. It had hinted at a comparison with Houser's nearly foot long. The Korean wasn't that long, but not far off, and he was thicker than Houser was.

"Do you ever dress as a woman . . . during sex?" the Korean asked.

"I haven't, but I will if that's what you want," Tyler said.

The Korean gave a low laugh. "Yes, you will do anything I want."

Tyler shuddered at that, and the Korean felt, and seemed to enjoy, that. He took two condom packets out of his pocket and slit them open with his teeth.

"So there will be no mess," he whispered, and he crowned, first Tyler, and then himself. He stroked Tyler's sheathed cock for a moment, while Tyler did the same with his. But then he was fondling the young man's balls.

"No noise now," he muttered. "Take it silently." He was squeezing and distending the balls, coming close to crushing them. There was that brief look of cruelty in his eyes again. Tyler writhed in his embrace, his eyes watering, but he controlled himself, not crying out.

"Good," the Korean said. He moved his hand lower and invaded Tyler's anus, deep, with first one finger and then another. He finger fucked Tyler's hole. Tyler was stroking both cocks now. And, silently, Tyler came inside his condom. Rhee folded the young man's sheathed cock back into his trousers and zipped him up. He lay back, still sideways, in his seat, observing Tyler's face with a slight, indulgent smile on his face while Tyler continued to slowly beat him off. He had admirable control. It took Tyler twenty minutes to bring the man to his orgasm.

They visited the lavatory separately to get rid of the condoms and clean up and to settle in for the night. They didn't settle in for the whole time, though. Two hours later, to the tune of light snores and everyone else in first class either snoozing or trying like hell to snooze, the Korean nudged Tyler awake. Rhee was unzipped and his cock was out, flopping long and thick against his thigh.

"Suck me off," he commanded, pulling the face of a half-asleep Tyler down into his lap. The young man kept his gagging and gurgling to the minimum he was able, as he unhinged his jaw, took as much of the cock as he could into his throat, and gave his new master an expert blow job. Again, the Korean exhibited admirable control, running his fingers into the young man's long, blond hair and moving the head up and down on the swallowed cock for more than fifteen minutes before he came down Tyler's throat in three prodigious jettings.

Leaning back into the corner of his seat next to the window, Tyler extracted a handkerchief from his pocket and wiped off his lips while Rhee folded a now-flaccid monster cock back into his fly and zipped himself up.

"Satisfactory. Quite satisfactory," the Korean whispered.

Aloha week had begun.

* * * *

A limousine drove them from the Honolulu airport to the Royal Hawaiian Waikiki hotel. A suite was awaiting them, and there was a box on a table in the suite's living room when they arrived, with one of the assistant managers saying, "This arrived for you yesterday, Mr. Rhee, and we took the liberty of putting it in your room."

"Thank you," Rhee said and stood there, fingering the box, until the assistant manager bowed his way out. Tyler explored the suite, arriving back by the Korean's side as Rhee was pulling a set of lacy black bikini panties, bra, garter belt, black mesh stockings, and black high heels out of the box.

"As you can see, I anticipated whether you would dress up for me. Lee shared your photograph, and I knew you'd be perfect for this role play. Here, strip down if you please and put these on. Lee said these would fit you."

As Tyler changed, without objection, Rhee was also stripping and adjusting a black leather harness on his chest, pulling on black boots, and snapping on black leather wrist bands, all of which came out of the box. The Korean was tall and slim and wiry. He was quite athletic too, and Tyler couldn't help but find him sexy. He couldn't object to being dominated by the man and that obviously was what this was all about.

Rhee pulled a hand whip out of the box, commanded, "Kneel to me," forcing Tyler, dressed in the bra and panties, to his knees in front of him with a cruel grip of his head hair. Rhee forced his huge cock between the young man's lips, and, whimpering, Tyler opened his mouth to the cock. Flicking the whip, Rhee controlled the bobbing of Tyler's head on his cock, with one hand buried in the hair on the back of the young man's head, and side-arm whipped the blond's buttocks, back, and thighs with the whip in the other hand. The lashes weren't brutal, but they stung a bit, and Tyler was sobbing when Rhee pulled his dick out of the young man's mouth after several minutes of face fucking, but no ejaculation yet.

"Do you want me to stop?" the Korean growled.

"Do what you want," Tyler responded through his tears.

"Right answer," Rhee said.

The Korean swept the box off the table with his arm, turned and pulled Tyler up from his knees, and slammed the young man down on his belly on the table. Tyler's legs were dangling off the other side of the table, not quite touching the floor. Rhee saddled up behind him, ripped the panties off his pelvis, and wishboned his legs cruelly straight out from his sides on either side. Tyler reached out to the side with both arms, clutching the table top on either side of him at the edge. Tyler's facial expression showed a mixture of shock, surprise, and arousal. The expression added in pain and passion, as the Korean worked his long, thick cock into the young whore's ass, taking all the time in the world to bottom as Tyler panted and moaned, and began bareback fucking him hard and deep. He remarked how tight Tyler was when he first penetrated him and then, with a laugh, how quickly the passage stretched and opened to his insistence. He was quite pleased with that.

Rhee, holding the young man's hips between his hands, fucked Tyler's ass for twenty minutes with a blissful, satisfied look on his face. When he was on the edge of coming, he reached up, grabbed a hank of the young man's blond curls, and arched the his torso back cruelly. Tyler cried out, not for the first time, "Oh, shit, oh, fuck! You're huge."

"Yes I am, but you're taking me nicely," came back. "And you're taking me now." Rhee leaned over the prone body plastered to the table top, took one of Tyler's earlobes in his teeth, and blasted him deep inside with cum.

When he pulled out of Tyler's ass, he pulled the young man's body with him and let him collapse to the carpet, panting and moaning.

He was still there after the Korean had showered, dressed in a fresh business suit, and left, saying, "Dinner will be at eight. Amuse yourself while I'm gone, but keep your cell phone with you and answer if I call."

Tyler dragged himself across the room toward the bathroom.

That was all within the first two hours of their arrival in Honolulu on day one of Aloha Week.

At 11:00 that night, Tyler lay on his back in the bed, his wrists bound above his head to the headboard, his legs spread and bent, while Rhee crouched over him, sliding ten thick inches deep inside him, holding as their eyes locked and Tyler whimpered and panted, docilely taking the cock deep. As the cock was slowly withdrawn, Tyler sighed and arched his back. A slow slide in followed as Tyler gasped. Out, sigh; in, gasp. Out, in. OutIn. OUTIN. With a cry of, "Shit, here it comes," Tyler ejaculated. After he had, the Korean picked up the pace of the fuck. It was still the long slide and long withdrawal, but the pace picked up, becoming ever faster. Tyler arched his back and cried out, "Yes. Yes! Fuck me!" and the Korean did just that, until, at 11:45, he came and rolled off Tyler. Tyler had come a second time.

At 1:15 a.m., Rhee rolled back on top of Tyler and slid his cock hard and deep into the quick of the young man. "Yes, yes!" Tyler cried out. "Fuck me!" and the Korean fucked him until nearly two.

69

At 4:00 a.m., the Korean rolled back on top of Tyler and slid his cock in hard and deep . . .

Thus ended night one of Aloha week.

* * * *

"Lopaka," Tyler said. The hunky Hawaiian hotel pool bar waiter had put the refill of Tyler's drink down on the table next to his pool bed, and Tyler asked the young man if he really was Hawaiian. He certainly looked it, all brown and muscular and sunny smile. He was wearing a colorful sarong-like wrap around his waist, a lei of white orchids around his neck, and was barefoot. When the young man—not as young as Tyler but not more than four years older—had affirmed he was a native Hawaiian, Tyler had asked him if he had an Hawaiian name.

"Yes," he'd said. "It's Lopaka. It means 'brilliant fame.' My parents were very optimistic, you see."

"Lopaka. I would say that your parents could read the future," Tyler said. "You are a beautiful man. I got a glimpse of the torch performance on the beach last night. You dance great. You're a very sexy man." It was Tyler's third drink. He'd been at the pool most of the afternoon, stretched out on the pool bed in a Brazilian cut micro bikini, which essentially was only a pouch and a thin string. He and this pool server had exchanged some interested glances before, and Tyler had seen the young man kissing a man who was older than they were and who'd been at the pool much of the afternoon. They had a quickie kiss in the bushes where they presumably didn't think anyone had seen them. The man was on a pool bed across the pool, and the attendant, Lopaka, had visited him several times, not always to deliver a drink. Sometimes it was just to banter. The man obviously wanted more than drinks from Lopaka.

"It's pronounced 'Lo-pa-ka,' with an emphasis on the 'pa,'" the attendant said. "And I know you watched me a bit last evening. You should see the whole show."

"I hope to see it all tonight," Tyler said.

"If you want to see 'it all,' I would be happy to show it," Lopaka said, giving Tyler a wink. Both young me gave a low laugh at that.

Lopaka sat down on the edge of the pool bed and placed a hand on Tyler's inner thigh. Tyler left it there. He had been worn out the night before by Song Rhee in bed, but he had awakened horny for more. Song Rhee was a master cocksman and Tyler couldn't get over how thick he was, how deep he could get, how frequently he could get it up and stick it in, and how much he could hold Tyler in thrall to his cock. Rhee hadn't seemed flagged at all. He'd bounced out of bed, showered while his breakfast arrived, eaten, dressed quickly, and left the suite, while Tyler had just lain there and watched him, his legs spread open, more than half hoping the Korean would come onto the bed and do him again.

"It wouldn't take much to see all of *you*, would it?" Lopaka said, scanning Tyler's nearly nude body. "You are a sexy young man too. I understand that you are in one of the suites, with an important Korean businessman."

"I don't know how important he is," Tyler said, "but, yes, we are in the same room."

"And in the same bed, I do think. Don't give me that look. I think we are in the same business. You keep men like the Korean businessman happy and I keep the guests happy. Perhaps you might be interested in me keeping you happy for a bit this afternoon." He had pulled a room card out of a slit pocket in his sarong with one hand. The other hand was cupping Tyler's cock through the pouch of his micro bikini. Tyler was hardening, but he didn't brush the hand away.

"You're making a sweeping assumption, aren't you?" Tyler asked. He put a hand on top of the one that Lopaka was cupping his balls with.

"I don't think so," the Hawaiian responded, taking Tyler's hand, moving it into the folds of his sarong, and placing it on his own cock. He then put his hand back on Tyler's basket. "The way you look at me; the way you walk; what you wear, putting yourself on display as you do; being in the room and on the expense account of an older man, what the waiter saw when he delivered breakfast to your room this morning—it all screams 'Fuck me.' You can feel what I'm packing. You would be happy to have me fuck you, wouldn't you?"

"You are assuming that the Korean fucks me— that I don't top him."

"And my assumption is right, isn't it?"

"Yes. I'm always happy to have a young stud like you between my legs," Tyler said, with a laugh, "But who would be paying who?" He didn't take the proffered room card.

Lopaka shrugged. "We could write it off as professional courtesy going both directions." His smile was mesmerizing. "Maybe a training session. I bet I know some positions you haven't tried before."

"Not today, I don't think," Tyler said, and now he did withdraw his hands from the folds of the sarong and take Lopaka's hand and move it away. "I'm tired today."

"Because of what the Korean did to you last night? The room waiter said the sheets on your bed looked like a hurricane had gone through your room, and that you were sprawled on the bed like you'd been in the same hurricane."

"Yes, because of what the Korean did to me last night. And did to me again and again." Tyler smiled.

"What has he got that I don't besides money?"

"He's got a lot of money but he's also got ten thick inches. You don't. But yours is nice too. I'll think about it."

"Don't think too long," Lopaka said. Tyler could see that the Hawaiian stud was a bit stung by the length comparison. He stood and walked around the pool to the pool bed of the older man, who was perhaps in his late thirties and looked like a male model. He was slender, achingly handsome, and he had been walking around the pool and moving his body in somewhat of an effeminate manner. Tyler gave a little laugh when he saw Lopaka pass the room card to the other man, who palmed it.

Ten minutes later, the other man rose from his pool bed and walked to a path at the edge of the hotel that wound around to the lawn above the beach. For curiosity sake, Tyler rose from his pool bed when he saw Lopaka take the path too, and followed him.

Others at the pool had been ogling Tyler, and when he came around to the other side of the pool, tailing Lopaka, a hand reached out and grabbed his wrist. Two men, good bodies both, lay on side-by-side pool beds. The one who had grabbed Tyler's wrist was a white guy, probably in his early fifties, all wavy gray hair on his head, curly salt-and-pepper on his chest and belly, and a smile, but a good body for his age. the other one was a younger black guy, probably in his mid forties and profoundly muscular, smooth bodied, and rich chocolate brown. The white guy was well tanned and both were wearing pouch bikinis. The black guy's pouch bulged obscenely. The black guy had his hand on his bulge.

"Whoa, where do you have to be so urgently, blondie? Ray and I here—I'm Doug; we're here to golf in the PGA tournament—have been watching you. You look lonely. Ray and I think you could use a little companionship."

"Companionship would cost the two of you $500," Tyler said flippantly, just to be able to move on. "You got $500 in that pouch of yours?"

"Ah, a rent-boy. I knew it. Ray wasn't so sure. You'd be amazed at what Ray's got in that pouch of his."

"Not rent; more like on contingency," Tyler said. "Nice meeting you, though. I've got to see a man about a man now." Tyler pulled away and pointed himself in the direction Lopaka had gone.

"Maybe next time Ray and me will have that $500 in our pouches. Bet you're first rate for that money. You're a sexy little thing. Been sexing up that pool boy."

"Fine, show me the money," Tyler said and started down the path around the side of the building. Funny, he thought, he hadn't hesitated to say he'd go with them, although he'd named a godawful amount just to change their minds. Not so funny that they

74

recognized immediately what he would do for a man. He'd always seen taking sailors on Guam as something on the side to augment his income. Guess he was in the big time now. He'd have to think about what that meant to him. For now, though, he was curious.

The path led around to a string of ground-floor rooms opening onto patios and the grassy area at the top of the hotel's share of the beach. Heavy foliage helped block the view from the lawn into the rooms.

Tyler found that he could position himself in the shrubbery so that he could look into the hotel room Lopaka had entered. He wasn't surprised to see the man from pool lying on his back, naked, on the bed, his legs bent and spread. He had a beautiful, sleek body and an all-over tan. When Tyler looked into the room, he saw Lopaka standing at the foot of the bed, untying the sarong at his waist. When it dropped to the floor, Lopaka was revealed to be naked and in magnificent erection. Whereas the body of the other man was sleek and willowy, Lopaka was muscular. They both were deeply tanned, but Lopaka's tan came more from his Hawaiian ancestry.

Lopaka went down between the other man's spread legs, covering him, and Tyler could tell from the expression of the man that the Hawaiian was sucking his cock and eating out his asshole. The man was holding Lopaka's head in his hands, writhing under Lopaka's attentions, and running his mouth off saying things that didn't reach Tyler where he was in the shrubbery. After a good ten minutes of preparing the man, Lopaka rose up, moved over the man's body between his spread legs, penetrated him, and began to pump him. The man moved his body with the thrusts.

Now Tyler was able to hear him mouthing off his passion at the fuck he was receiving.

Lopaka fucked the man for nearly twenty minutes. Tyler was able to discern the exact second that each of the men ejaculated. So engrossed had he been in the fuck scene that he didn't realize that he had been pulling on his own cock through the pouch of his bikini or that he had come in the pouch.

When Song Rhee returned to the suite a bit after 5:00 p.m., Tyler pounced on him, taking them both to the floor, tore at the Korean's trousers until he had freed the man's cock, sucked him hard, saddled his hips over the man's pelvis, skewered himself on the cock, and rode it hard. If the Korean chose to think Tyler was turned on thinking of him. That was OK with Tyler, but he actually was horny from watching the Hawaiian fucking the other man in the garden room. Laughing, Rhee grabbed the young man by the hips and slammed him up and down on his cock to a mutual ejaculation.

"This doesn't mean that I let you off from the fuck tonight," Rhee said when they'd both come.

"I hope not," Tyler said. "But I have a request. I want to watch the native torch ceremony they do down on the beach at 8:00 p.m. again—this time all the way through."

At 10:00 p.m. that night, Tyler was suspended over the carpet, facing the ceiling. His arms were raised over his head behind him, his hand grasping the edge of the table in the suite's living room. His body streamed forward to the Korean's, who was standing in a crouch between the young man's thighs, his hands holding the blond's body up by clutching his waist. Tyler's ankles were locked at the small of Rhee's back, and the Korean's hands were pulling the young man's buttocks back and forth on his cock. This athletic fuck transitioned into the Korean lying on his back on the table with the young blond whore suspended over his body in a crab position, Tyler's hands and feet flat on the table on either side of the Korean's body and his pelvis rising and falling on the Korean's cock.

At midnight, Tyler was sitting at a vanity table brushing out his hair. He was wearing a silk robe. Song Rhee, also in a robe, came over and stood behind Tyler, placing his hands on Tyler's shoulders.

"I had a difficult deal to make today," the Korean said. "I had to make a concession."

Tyler looked up at him through the mirror over the vanity table. He didn't ask what sort of deal or what concession. He just waited for Rhee to tell him whatever he would—and maybe why he was telling Tyler anything.

"His named is Jack. He's an Aussie, and he can, I think, be a bit crude." One of Rhee's hands came around the side of Tyler and a hotel room card dropped on the vanity table. "I have given you to him for the night."

The Aussie was big, with crude, ruddy features. He'd probably been a power rugby player in his day. It hadn't been his day for a good fifteen years, though, and although still muscular and strong, he had excess poundage.

He also applied excess poundage to Tyler, bouncing the young man around in the bed in his less-plush hotel room through the night. Slapping the young man around and riding him hard and constantly.

Thus ended day two of the Aloha week.

* * * *

When the Australian thug left for meetings in the morning, Tyler dragged back to the suite, soaked for an hour in the tub, slept until two, ordered a lunch from room service, and was at the pool, stretched out on his pool bed, wearing his micro pouch bikini at 3:00 p.m.

At 3:15 p.m. Lopaka passed by for a drink order and, when Tyler shook his head, the waiter pulled the hotel room card out of his pocket and gave Tyler a quizzical look. Tyler nodded his assent and Lopaka, with a laugh, dropped the room card on the table next to Tyler's pool bed.

At 3:30 p.m. the hunky Hawaiian gigolo was sitting on the foot of the bed in the hotel garden room Tyler had seen him perform in the previous day, with Tyler, facing away from him, in his lap, his torso cantilevered over the carpet like a figurehead on a sailing ship, his legs streaming around and in back of Lopaka's hips, his arms stretched back, his wrists grasped in Lopaka's hands, and the Hawaiian's cock mining the depths of the young whore's channel.

The Hawaiian was barebacking Tyler. Tyler no longer gave a shit about that.

At 4:00 p.m. Tyler was on his belly on the bed. Lopaka also was on his belly, but reversed on Tyler's body, the Hawaiian's legs hugging Tyler's torso and his cock buried, reversed, in Tyler's passage. The Hawaiian was rocking back and forth, fucking Tyler's hole.

The Hawaiian had said he wanted to try out exotic positions "with another professional." Tyler was game.

Tyler had barely managed to get back to the suite when Song Rhee returned for the day. He brought the Aussie, Jack, with him. Rhee sat across the suite's bedroom and watched as the Aussie stretched his body beside Tyler's, Tyler on his back, with his right leg raised painfully straight up his body, his ankle trapped behind the Aussie's neck, while, with a greased hand, the Aussie stuffed the hand up to the knuckles in Tyler's ass and hand fucked him, while Tyler huffed and puffed and did a little silent howling. Growing tired of threatening to put the whole fist inside Tyler but not quite carrying through, the Aussie rolled over on top of Tyler, thrust his cock up into Tyler's now-gaping hole, and fucked him hard, cruelly, and at great length while he wrapped his fists around Tyler's throat and controlled the young man's ability to get breath.

It must have been quite a concession the Korean was granting this man, Tyler thought.

After dinner, Song Rhee went off clubbing in downtown Honolulu with the men he was holding business negotiations with. They didn't take Tyler with them, and Tyler went to bed early.

He woke at 3:00 a.m. to the sensation of being in a rocking boat. Rhee was fucking a young transvestite on the bed next to him. Tyler could tell the transvestite was impressed with the length and thickness of the Korean's cock. His painted face was turned toward Tyler's and Tyler could tell the Korean had his full attention from the gasp that escaped the transvestite when Rhee was taking the long slide deep inside him, the look of pain-pleasure-passion when the cock bottomed, and then the hissing sigh as the cock was pulled back.

Tyler dozed off. At 4:15 a.m. he was awakened by feeling Song Rhee climb on top of him, turning him on his belly, coaxing him up a bit on his knees, mounting his ass, and driving his cock inside. Then it was Tyler who was gasping at the sinking of the cock and sighing at its withdrawal. The transvestite lay there beside them, moaning.

At 5:00 a.m., the Korean transferred his attention to the transvestite again.

Thus ended day three of the Aloha week.

* * * *

Tyler woke up at 10:00 a.m. He was alone in the bed. The transvestite was gone. The sheets were so messed up, the bedspread half on the floor, that the bed looked like a battle zone. He almost laughed, remembering what Lopaka had said the waiter who delivered breakfast the previous day had said about that. Tyler wasn't sure but he thought maybe he'd been sucked and fucked by the transvestite sometime in the night as well as by Song Rhee. He had bits of pancake makeup on his face, neck, and his inner thighs.

Rhee was moving around the suite's bedroom, packing a small bag.

"Going someplace?" Tyler asked in a groggy voice.

"Something's happened. We suspect surveillance," Rhee answered cryptically. "We've rented a charter boat. Going out to international waters. Overnight. I'll be back tomorrow evening. Find something to occupy yourself with."

"I can't go with you?" Tyler asked.

"No. Some of the people I'm talking to are antsy about who knows what. No outsiders."

OK, Tyler thought. It sounds like I don't want to know what that's about. And I did my duty and asked. Luckily, Rhee didn't specify what he couldn't do in terms of finding something to occupy him. He turned over in the bed and snoozed.

At 11:00 he ordered brunch brought to the room. He remembered to straighten up the bed before the waiter arrived. At noon he was out at the pool, stretched out on a pool bed, somewhat disappointed because his drink wasn't served by Lopaka.

"Lopaka?" the older guy who served his drink said. "This is his day off."

Tyler settled down in a pout, picking up a porn book he'd ordered from Amazon, *Tramp Steamer*, about a guy being fucked all over the South Pacific. Tyler was enjoying the book—his kind of guy. Some couldn't understand how you could lie on your back and open your legs to a variety of cocks, one after the other, but, like this guy in the book, Tyler never felt more alive than when there was a stud—or a guy with money—humping him and the next guy standing behind, waiting his turn. That's probably, Tyler thought, why he was drifting further into prostitution.

He sensed someone was there by the shadow that passed over the book he was reading. It was two someones, though, in their pouch bikinis, as was Tyler. Doug, the older white guy, sat down on the pool bed to Tyler's right. He had a wad of money in his left hand. His right hand came down on the inner thigh of Tyler's right leg.

"Five hundred?" Tyler asked.

"Five hundred," Doug said and smiled. Ray, the black bull, sat down on the pool bed to Tyler's left. He placed a hand on the inner thigh of Tyler's left leg. "How easy are you willing to be?"

"I can be very easy for $500," Tyler said.

"This easy?" Doug said, moving his hand up Tyler's thigh and touching his cockhead through the material of the pouch with his thumb.

"Oh, I can be a lot easier than that." He pulled the pouch of his bikini down and hooked it under his balls, letting the man press his thumb into his piss slit. He pulled Doug's face down to his and they kissed. Tyler opened his lips to Doug's tongue.

"OK with taking us both?" Doug asked, after coming out of the kiss. He was playing with Tyler's balls with his hand and Tyler was letting him. "It's a lot of money. It's for us both."

"You both? Sure, one after the other. No problem. But that's not what you mean, is it?"

"No, that's not what I mean. Together. At the same time. You OK with it? You can handle it?"

Tyler paused for a moment. Ray was probably a monster. Doug probably not. While he contemplated, both of the men were nudging his legs open and raising and bending them. Doug was rolling his balls in his hand. Tyler began to pant. It wasn't just the money. He liked to be fucked. And $500. He figured that Rhee was paying him nearly $750 just to be here today. And Rhee wasn't even here today. $1,250 a day and just these two guys, even if together. He was really moving up into the money. He didn't do anything about Doug grasping and rolling his balls—other than moaning for him, so Ray had his hand on his dick and was slow stroking it.

"Or $300 for us one at a time, if you won't do a double. But more than once each," Doug said.

Tyler had done doubles before, once or twice, with sailors. It had hurt but he'd managed them. And they hadn't paid him any $500 to do it, either. "I think we can do the five hundred," he said, "but you think you're going to do me right here, now, at the pool, with others around the pool?"

"Naw," Doug said, with a smile. "I'm pretty anxious. I want to do you here, in the bushes maybe, for starters. Then we'll move it upstairs. Your room or one of ours?"

"You're not in the same room?"

"Of course not," Doug said, with a grin. "What do you think we are? A couple of homos?"

All three of them laughed.

"Mine," Tyler said. That way he could maintain some semblance of control over this. "But here? Now?"

"Sure," Doug said, looking around. He smiled, showed that he had a couple of condom packets in the hand along with the wad of money, and tossed one of them to Ray, who grabbed it out of the air with the hand he wasn't stroking Tyler's cock with.

Doug put Tyler on all fours in the bushes not ten feet from his pool bed. He spent a few minutes, but not much time, with his face buried in Tyler's crack and a hand under Tyler's belly, pulling on the young man's cock. Ray went down on his haunches next to them and watched. In no time, though, Doug was hunched over Tyler, high on the young man's buttocks, grasping Tyler's hips, and fucking him in long slides. Tyler took over pulling on his own cock, but Ray reached under there, brushing Tyler's hand away, taking over the stroking, and milked Tyler to a finish while Doug kept on humping him.

When Doug was done and had pulled out, Ray assumed the position, Tyler looking around to see the brown hands slide up his ribs and hold there. Tyler fought hard not to cry out. The black bull was bigger than the older white man was in every way. And he was stronger, more forceful, more vigorous. Tyler gritted his teeth and writhed a bit under the black man's controlling embrace, as Ray took him hard and deep.

"Lookee here, Doug," Ray called out. "A hole in one."

"The surprise is that the hole could take that driver you got," Doug answered, and laughed. "It's a sweet hole, and tight."

"It ain't tight anymore," Ray said.

And that was the truth.

Upstairs, on the bed in the suite, Doug lay on his back, legs descending to the floor at the foot of the bed, and Tyler kneeling and sitting on his cock, facing him. Hands grasping the older man's torso just above the waistline, Tyler was doing a cowboy, rising and falling on the white man's cock, when Ray saddled in behind him, pushed Tyler's chest forward, onto the salt-and-pepper matting of Doug's heaving chest, worked his shaft inside Tyler's ass as Tyler mouthed off about how impossibly big he was, and started to pump.

Ray was pounding him hard, when the black bull came up on the edge of the bed on his knees, trapping Tyler's knees between his and Doug's thighs, grabbed Tyler's wrists, cantilevered their bodies back over the carpet from Doug's chest, and set his buttocks in motion, pounding, pounding, and pounding Tyler's ass, rocking them both back and forth on Doug's buried cocks. It wasn't long before orgasms were had all around.

The men got thirds, each of them riding Tyler's ass with him on his belly on the bed. He was exhausted and drifting off to sleep when they left. When he woke and stirred, he felt the bills on his back. They had scattered the $500 in bills on his bare back in the bed. He moaned. He'd earned that $500.

The next thing he knew he heard, "What the hell is this? Is this how the Korean pays you?"

Lopaka, in shorts, a loose Hawaiian shirt—which only Hawaiians could wear well without deserving a snicker—and sandals, was standing by the bed.

"Maybe," Tyler said, adding, "What's it to you? I hope you're not here to fuck me right at this moment."

Lopaka's hand went to Tyler's crack. "Holy shit, you're open enough that a Mac truck could have been up there. You told me the Korean was monster hung, but—"

"He is," Tyler said, cutting him off because he didn't want to admit to taking money from two men for a shared fuck while another man was giving him money to fuck him. He might be that much of a slut, but he didn't want to broadcast it. "How did you get in here, and isn't this your day off?"

"I can get a master key when I want it, and I heard that your Korean has gone out on the ocean overnight. I thought you'd enjoy the company. I thought you'd like to see the island for the day and not be cooped up here all day. You want to play tourist for a few hours?"

"Does playing tourist involve your dick?"

"It could if you play your cards right," Lopaka said, with a laugh. "But I thought you might like to see how Hawaiians really live."

"Oh, hell, why not? I've already felt how Hawaiians really fuck," Tyler said, rolling out from underneath his early afternoon winnings and putting his feet on the floor. "You want to fuck me first?"

Lopaka laughed. "Of course, but I won't. All in good time. I want you to shower and find something to wear that won't have the locals falling on you to rape you, and then I want to walk you up a volcano."

Tyler padded off to the bathroom, while Lopaka gathered up his doubles money in a nice neat stack for him.

Lopaka took Tyler touring on Oahu from under the sea—the Atlantis Submarine tour off Waikiki—to Pearl Harbor at the western end of the beach to the top of a dormant volcano, Diamond Head, at the eastern end. Then he drove him in his Jeep up to the top of the Koola Mountain Range for a view down into Honolulu. It was late afternoon by the time they got up there, and Lopaka hadn't laid a hand on the young man. It probably was the longest Tyler had gone unfucked since he'd landed on Oahu. They laughed and chatted and stopped and ate here and there, though. It was an exhausting, but fun-filled, day. Still, each time Lopaka touched Tyler, it sent a charge of electricity through the young man and brought up visions of the exotic positions in which the Hawaiian had taken him. Each time he wanted to whimper, "Fuck me. Take me someplace exotic and fuck me." It wasn't lost on him that he was sinking into the need for the cock.

When they left the Koola Mountains, they started descending to the east rather than to the south.

"This isn't the way we came up into the mountains," Tyler said.

"No it isn't. You don't have to be back at the hotel tonight. I don't want you sleeping in the Korean's bed tonight, even if he's not there. I want you to sleep in my bed. And I want you to experience how Hawaiians really live. I want you to meet my family. They're your kind of people. I have to be at work tomorrow morning; I'll have you back in the hotel before your Korean can return."

"But how will they—your family—?" Tyler was wondering what being his "kind of the family" meant.

"They know I go with men. They will treat you like family. Always." Tyler looked over sharply at the young Hawaiian when he said the "always." Tyler didn't ask about that. He wasn't sure he wanted to know what Lopaka meant by that. It started him thinking about possibilities that had never occurred to him before, however.

They drove down from the mountains into Kanelohe Bay and then north, along the shore of the bay, to near the end, just beyond a town named Walkane. Lopaka's family lived in a compound of simple houses in the foliage above the beach. Lopaka had a small house all his own. Tyler was inundated with family when they arrived. He concentrated on the men, Lopaka's brothers and uncles, his father having passed, mainly because they were all such hunks. They were all wearing just colorful sarongs around their waists. It was getting dark when Lopaka and Tyler arrived, and the men of the family were roasting a pig down on the beach to have a luau.

"My brother Kai and his boyfriend Akamai; my brothers Tua and Kahili; my uncles Henale and Haulani and Moana." The introductions went on like that, overwhelming Tyler. He hadn't gotten much beyond the surprise of a brother with an openly declared boyfriend. No one seemed to mind. There was a mother and a few sisters and aunts too, and a grandmother, but Tyler didn't really zone in on anyone but the hunky men. The women did seem to fade into the background. This was a manly sort of family. Tyler wondered if that's what Lopaka had meant by this being Tyler's kind of family.

There was a luau by a bonfire on the beach after dark and Hawaiian music and dancing and torch juggling. Performing for the tourists seemed to be a family business, and they were all graceful—and sexy at it. Tyler sat, between Lopaka's legs, his back into Lopaka's chest, both of them wearing just sarongs as they watched the dancing—whenever Lopaka wasn't up there dancing as well. They were drinking some sort of potent home brew too.

"Some of your brothers and uncles look familiar," Tyler said. He had to repeat that, though, because he was slurring his words a bit from the drink.

"They should," Lopaka said. "Some of them work at the Royal Hawaiian Waikiki, just like I do. And they, like I, often perform in the hotel's evening torch dance."

They were near the fringe of the light from the bonfire, and Lopaka was holding Tyler close into his body. Slowly couples were pairing off and receding into the foliage to fuck. One brother, Tua, was fucking one of the young women, one uncle, Kahili, one of the hunkiest men there, was fucking one of the young men who had been turning the pig on the spit when Lopaka and Tyler had arrived. Akamai was riding the cock of

Lopaka's brother, Kai. The uncle Henale had a woman under him. Another uncle, Moana, was fucking a young man Tyler hadn't been introduced to. A man, who had been given some deference when he came strolling down the beach and invited to the luau on the fly was fucking Lopaka's mother. When one brother or uncle was finished when a young man or women, they passed them on to the next. It was a regular Hawaiian orgy. All of them had beautiful bodies.

Ah so, Tyler thought. *This* was what Lopaka meant when he said this was Tyler's sort of family.

Tyler could feel the hardening of Lopaka's cock at the small of his back. He turned his face to the Hawaiian and they kissed deeply. Lopaka was running his hands of over Tyler's chest and the young man was moaning as Lopaka buried his face in the hollow of Tyler's throat; reached down and unknotted the young man's sarong, brushing the two sides open; fisted Tyler's cock; and, as Tyler writhed in his grip, beat the young man's shaft to an ejaculation to the rhythm of the drum someone was beating on the beach. Lopaka reclined onto his back in the sand, taking Tyler with him; skewered the young man's passage on his cock; grasped, raised, and spread Tyler's legs; and raised and lowered Tyler on his cock to his own ejaculation.

At last, raced through Tyler's mind. He'd been aching for a fuck. "Yes! Fuck me!" he cried out, and in the surrounding foliage, the words echoed around the other copulating couples. "Fuck me hard!" "Fuck me harder!" "Fuck me hardest!"

"I'm going to take you into my hut now," Lopaka whispered in Tyler's ear, and Tyler muttered something incomprehensible in return. Lopaka rose, picked Tyler up in his arms, and carried the young man across the threshold of his hut and to his bed. He fucked Tyler again, sitting on the foot of his bed, with Tyler in his lap, on his cock, and facing him.

"Arch back and grab my ankles," Lopaka commanded, and Tyler did so. The hunky Hawaiian pulled the young man on and off his cock to a mutual ejaculation. After a short rest, he took Tyler in a side-split on the bed. A lot of cuddling, kissing, and fondling transpired after this fuck. Lopaka was growing more and more affectionate with Tyler. Tyler wasn't used to getting this kind of attention from a man and he thought it was cute—and maybe a bit disconcerting as well. They both dozed then, after Tyler whispered in Lopaka's ear, "Do you know what I want?"

"I always know what you want. You want the cock."

"Yes, but you know what else I want?" But he didn't tell Lopaka what that was. Instead, he drifted off to sleep in Lopaka's arms and dreamt about what he really wanted.

Tyler was back down on the beach, in the dark, the area around him lit eerily by torches. Lopaka was under him, his cock buried up Tyler's channel. Tyler was lying on top of him and Lopaka held his legs spread and raised. One after the other, first the brothers Tua, Henale, and Kai, in ascending cock order, and then the uncles, Moana, Haulani, and Kahili, even greater bulls, knelt between Tyler's legs, penetrated him above Lopaka's buried cock, and pumped him full of cum. They were exhausting him. Cum was running out of his hole. He was moaning deeply.

Then without transition, he was sitting, sideways in one of the hammocks that were dotted around the family compound. But he was bound, his arms stretched wide, restraints on his wrists leading to the two trees the hammock was attached to. His legs similarly were raised and spread, tied off at the ankles to two other trees. Lopaka was behind him, embracing him. Lopaka's cock was pressing into the small of Tyler's back. A succession of men: Kai, Tua, Moana, Henale, Haulani, Kahili, even the older man who had come down the beach and covered Lopaka's mother, were moving in between his legs, penetrating him, fucking him. When they'd been through the rotation, it started all over again. Tyler was writhing for them, but crying out in passion. They all were impossibly hung. They all had cocks that slithered in his passage like snakes. He shot off again and again and again.

He woke to geysering an arc of cum up into Lopaka's stomach. His arms were stretched over his head, restraints on his wrists leading to the corner posts at the head of the bed. His legs were raised and spread, the ankles restrained by leads going to hooks in the ceiling. The Hawaiian stud was crouched between his legs, pulling him on and off his cock with strong hands on his hips. It was nearly dawn outside. They would have to leave soon to make it to the hotel before Lopaka's shift started.

"You bound me and then fucked me," Tyler said accusingly.

"Repeatedly. I fucked you repeatedly," Lopaka answered in a calm voice.

"Why am I bound?"

"You asked for it. Don't you remember? Were you that drunk last night? You saw the hooks in the ceiling and the restraints and the corner posts and you said you wanted to be bound and ravished. I gave you what you said you wanted. You also said you wanted to invite my brothers and uncles in to fuck you too, but

I'm not that much into sharing. I want you all to myself."

"Do you often bring young men home to share with your family?"

"Well, not often. Yes, we all do occasionally. But I made clear to my brothers and uncles that you are special. You are mine. Akamai was one of those who Kahili brought back and we trussed him up right where you are and we fucked the stuffing out of him—every man here who wanted to fuck him did so. He was willing; he'd come here as a rent-boy. Kai liked him so much he kept him."

"You mean the heaviest hung of all of you, your uncle Kahili, could come in here with me bound like this and fuck me silly if I was willing?"

"Well, no, I've already told them that you're off limits . . . that you're just for me."

"Oh. You know that really makes me feel horny. You know what I'd like—"

"Time for us to get rolling to work," Lopaka said, starting to free Tyler. "Everyone else has already left for work. Time for us to get on the road too."

"Oh, um. OK."

Day four of Aloha week had ended and they were moving into day five.

* * * *

Lopaka let Tyler off a block from the entrance to the Royal Hawaiian so that they wouldn't be linked by the hotel reception desk. Tyler was stopped at the desk and handed a note, which told him he had an appointment at the health spa for a treatment and a massage at 3:00 p.m. that day.

"It must be some mistake," Tyler said. "I haven't made a spa appointment."

"It was made by Mr. Rhee," the man at the desk said. "And charged to his room. Is that not your room too?"

The clerk was looking down his nose at Tyler, a knowing expression on his face. He knew that Rhee was keeping Tyler in his suite for sex. It was a big, popular, five-star hotel. They were accustomed to accommodating the Song Rhees of the world. He wouldn't stand in judgment—although, of course, his very demeanor screamed that he was.

"OK," Tyler said, "But what's the treatment it mentions?"

"I wouldn't know, I'm sure," the clerk said.

"OK, thanks," Tyler said, giving the clerk a smile. The clerk was gay, so the smile from someone like Tyler was an ice melter and he changed on the spot, giving Tyler a comradely smile in return.

"I'm sure you will enjoy it, though," he confided.

As Tyler walked away, one of the other clerks leaned in and said, "Really nice tail on that one."

"Not my style," the first clerk said.

"That's because you're a bottom too. I wouldn't mind getting my cock in that. I understand that Lopaka has had him."

"I'll bet anyone with the price can have him," the first clerk said, and then, with a sniff, he turned to deal with another hotel guest.

On his way up to the suite, Tyler thought about—and worried about—Lopaka. He was a great top but it was getting too intense with him. And Tyler was disappointed that he hadn't taken the hint about a gang bang with Lopaka's brothers and uncles. They all were hunks. Of course, he realized what he should be worried about was how jaded and needy for cock he was becoming. As long as most of them paid big bucks for it, though . . .

He was at the suite, and he was exhausted. After a day of being horny and not getting it, Lopaka had given it to him again and again during the night. He was tired. He entered the suite, stripped down, took a shower, and hit the bed.

At 10:30, he heard the door of the suite open. He called out "Lopaka?" but luckily his throat had caught and the sound that had come out wasn't audible beyond the bed.

Because . . . it wasn't Lopaka, using a pass key, it was Song Rhee returning to the suite. And he was returning after a day and a half of not enjoying the charms of the little whore he was paying $750 a day for. He remedied that immediately, stripping down, climbing into the bed, and manhandling Tyler into a position where the young man was on his knees, on top of Rhee's prone body, the Korean holding and squeezing the young man's buttocks and eating out his ass, while Tyler leaned forward and did what he could to deep throat Rhee's cock.

The Korean moved Tyler into the position of hanging on to the top of the headboard to hold steady, and crouched over his tail working his cock into Tyler's passage. In deep—which in the Korean's case was ten thick inches of deep, and holding, while Tyler, his head arched back, his face set in the expression of a silent scream, fought hard to open enough to the buried cock for it to pump him. the Korean grasped Tyler's butt cheeks and spread them to pull his hole open as much as possible to take the thick cock. Out nearly all the way, to Tyler's sigh. In again, with Tyler gasping. And then innnn, out; innnn, out; INNNNOUT, and the Korean was pumping him fast and deep, Tyler's passage wall muscles rippling over the plunging shaft.

Tyler held, panting hard and grimacing at the depth the man was getting and the vigor with which he was pounding. He gave a long sigh when Rhee tensed and jerked several times in unleashing his spunk inside Tyler's passage. Tyler couldn't help himself. He'd been obsessed with the thought of Lopaka's super hung uncle, Kahili, fucking him since he'd know that was a possibility, and he surfaced his dream from the previous night while Rhee was finishing him off and thought of a Lopaka family gang bang with him as a trussed-up main dish.

The Korean bounded off the bed and went to the bathroom, for a piss, he said, when he was done. He remarked, though, that he wasn't finished getting his rocks off with Tyler and would be back—that they didn't have much time before they had to be at lunch.

Tyler went over to a window that overlooked the pool. They weren't on a floor too high for him not to be able to pick out Lopaka down there, in his sarong, delivering drinks to the hotel guests. Doug and Ray were down there too on their regular pool beds. A young man was sitting on the bed Doug was reclining on, talking with them. He was going to have a very sore ass in the near future, Tyler thought, and laughed a low laugh.

"What's funny?" Song Rhee asked, coming up behind Tyler and embracing him from behind. Tyler was surprised to be able to feel that Rhee was wearing the leather chest harness he'd worn on the first day here. And the leather wrist bands. He felt the swish of the whip cords on his leg.

"I want to be hard again fast," the Korean said. "Jut your ass back at me." The man's free hand palmed Tyler's lower belly, and Tyler jutted his buttocks back as commanded, emitting a little whimper, knowing where this was going. He raised his arms in front of him and placed his palms against the cool window. He pressed his cheek on the window as well and whimpered again at the sting of the first lash, not with a great deal of power behind it, but a sting none the less.

It only took four more lashes on his buttocks, with him sucking in breath, gasping, and whimpering at each sting of the whip, until Rhee was hard enough again to drop the whip, position his cockhead with his free hand, penetrate Tyler's ass a couple of inches and hold to move into his stance, and then pull back on the young man's belly while he thrust up inside Tyler's ass with his ten inches. In, out; innn, out; INNNOUT; and he was in business again.

Tyler looked down into the pool area. Lopaka was following some patron of the pool toward the path that went to the garden room he used to fuck the guests. Tyler could see down into the bushes behind the lines of pool beds. Doug and Ray weren't on their beds; they were in the bushes behind their beds. The young guy they'd been talking to was there too, on all fours. Doug, crouched over him, was riding his ass. Ray was on his haunches nearby, his hand reaching under the young guy's pelvis, no doubt milking his cock while Doug was doggie fucking the young man.

Life and sex went on.

"Get a fast shower and dress in something sexy but not too revealing for the dining room," Song Rhee said as he pulled out of Tyler's ass and slapped him on the butt. "We're dining with one of the men I'm dealing with—the last hurdle."

"A business lunch and you want me there?"

"I have to make another concession, a final one, I hope. If the man likes you, he'll be fucking you tonight. And if you pass with him at lunch, you'll have an appointment at the health spa at 3:00."

"And if he doesn't want me?" Tyler asked.

"Then you won't have to be body shaved at the spa. It's OK, you can keep the hair on your head. You can wear a skull cap."

Hey what? Body shaved?

* * * *

Tyler got the drift of what was happening and why over lunch in the hotel dining room. The man they met at the table was tall and big. He was a German named Gerhard, in his late forties or early fifties, and built like a bodybuilder. Notably, he was bald as a billiard ball. He wasn't just bald on his head. He had no eyebrows, no facial hair, no fuzz on his arms, no hair anywhere that Tyler could see. No hair on the tops of his feet, as Tyler was to find out as lunch was served. More notably, he was wearing gloves. They were ultrathin surgical gloves and weren't noticeable until you were close to him, but Tyler noticed them.

The luncheon talk was just chitchat, but it was obvious that Gerhard was testing Tyler out. They were in a booth, Gerhard across from Song Rhee and Tyler, Tyler against the wall. Gerhard was talking mostly to Rhee, but, under the table he was giving most of his attention to Tyler. He first lifted the young man's foot to his crotch, slipping off Tyler's sandal. Tyler wasn't wearing socks. The German had his fly open and his dick out and he ran the dick up the soles of Tyler's feet and between his toes. Tyler then took his turn holding the German bare foot into his exposed cock. The German ground his foot into Tyler's groin, and Tyler did what he could to smile at the man across the table.

At the end of the lunch, German pronounced to Rhee that he was pleased with the arrangement and he handed an extra pass key to his hotel room to Tyler, giving the young man a wink of his eyebrowless eye.

"You may keep your head hair," he said. "I rather like the feminine effect of it. No other trace of hair on your body, though," he said and then he was gone.

"You heard him," Rhee said. "If he signs on, we will be finished here. I'll add $1,000 to your fee if you please him and he signs. Your spa appointment is in half an hour. Regretfully I don't have time to use you before then. I'm feeling victorious. I could do so much to you at this moment. I think I'll make a phone call."

Tyler shuddered as the Korean slid out of the booth and walked away. Some poor young man was going to get worked over good.

∗ ∗ ∗ ∗

Tyler was disconcerted off the top when he went to the health spa at 3:00 to find that the person leading him back to a room with a shallow tub and a massage table in it was no other than Lopaka's Uncle Kahili. He probably shouldn't have been all that surprised, as Lopaka had said some of his brothers and uncles were in the hotel business, including working at the Royal Hawaiian.

Either Lopaka had failed to tell Kahili that Tyler was hands off or the uncle ignored the warning, because he was feeling Tyler's ass up as they walked back to the spa room.

He leaned his head into Tyler's head and whispered, "Lopaka's brought a lot of nice lays home to us but you by far were the best. He fucked you good and you took it great. He usually shares. I don't know why he didn't last night. You had me all hot and bothered. Still do."

"I kept thinking of you too and what your family does for fun with guys you bring home. I was sorry it didn't get into a gang bang too."

"You'd do it with us?"

"In an instant."

As they approached the room, Kahili ran his hand inside the back of Tyler's shorts and had the pad of his index finger pressed to Tyler's hole. "Do you mind?" he whispered into Tyler's ear.

"Do it," Tyler answered in a breathy voice.

Kahili propelled them into the room and pressed Tyler up against the wall by the door. He locked the door from the inside and then he was back at Tyler, holding the young man's cheek against the wall with one beefy hand and fingering the young man's rim with the other. Tyler yelped when Kahili's finger penetrated him.

"You OK with this?" Kahili asked.

"Do it," Tyler said and his eyes began to water and he gasped, as the Hawaiian stud entered him with another finger and finger fucked him.

"We've got plenty of time. I wish I could . . ."

"Do it. Do it now," Tyler hissed through chattering teeth.

Kahili fucked him in a plastic chair. Tyler was slouched in the chair, legs hung over the arms, and was pulling on his cock, while Kahili crouched over him, squeezing and separating the young man's butt cheeks, and ramming hard up into him with a championship cock. That was one talented cock too. It filled Tyler and coaxed Tyler's walls to undulate over it as it found every cranny and crevice in the anal passage and caressed, pounded, and conquered it.

"Good," he said, pushing himself off the young man when he'd released his cum in a condom. "I wanted to do that last night. You get Lopaka to bring you home tonight we'll all get together and bang you better than you've ever had before."

"I wanted you to do it last night too," Tyler answered. And, in his dreams the men of Lopaka's family *had* done it to him. He wondered how he could get away from Song Rhee to go back to the Hawaiian village that night—and how Lopaka could be convinced to share with his family.

"Now, hop up on this water table," Kahili said. "I don't know why you'd want this beautiful blond-haired body to be totally hairless, but if that's what's wanted . . ."

Tyler lay there, quickly hard again because the man shaving him down was hard again too and in the nude and had just fucked him to heaven, while Kahili lathered him up and shaved him down. The shave was much more intimate because they had been intimate. Tyler moaned throughout. Kahili milked Tyler every fifteen minutes, as soon as he was able to go hard again. While he was shaving down from Tyler's belly into his pubes, he was leaning over Tyler from the head of the water table. Tyler's head was arched over the head of the table and he sucking the Hawaiian stud off. Kahili lowered his head over Tyler's body and gave the young man head. When Kahili was shaving around Tyler's anal opening, he lathered up his middle finger and penetrated Tyler's ass, giving him a finger fuck while stroking off the young man's cock with the other hand.

No one got the A-1 sensual body shave that Tyler got from Lopaka's uncle. Tyler almost considered having to have one worthwhile.

When he was hairless except for what was on his head, Kahili dried him off with a towel, transferred him to the massage table and gave him a sensual massage that included Tyler sucking Kahili's cock with his head turned to the side while Kahili jacked Tyler's cock off.

"Do you want anything else?" the Hawaiian brute asked when Tyler had come.

"You know what I want, don't you?" Tyler said. "Didn't I see that this table had wrist and ankle restraints?"

He had, indeed, seen that. Tyler's wrists were tied down on either side of the massage table and his feet were restrained in stirrups on the side of the table that made him raise his tail high off the table. Kahili climbed up on the table, mounted Tyler ass, and fucked him into the next hour. finished, he leaned over and whispered in Tyler's ear, "Have Lopaka bring you out to the beach again so the brothers and uncles can fuck you good."

"That would be lovely," Tyler whispered.

At 5:00 p.m. Tyler was out at the pool, taking in the rays, and sighing from memories of Kahili's glorious cock.

Lopaka came out with a drink on a tray for Tyler than he hadn't ordered but took anyway.

"I heard you were at the spa today getting shaved down. Why a shave down?"

"Song Rhee wanted it. He had someone I'm supposed to sleep with who wants it that way. I think he's a hygiene nut."

"Do you do everything Song Rhee wants?"

"When he's paying the bill, yes."

"My uncle, Kahili, works at the spa. Is he the one who shaved you?"

"Yes, now that you mention it. I think it was one of your uncles."

"Did he get funny with you?"

"No, of course not." There was nothing funny about it. It was all business. Glorious business.

"I don't want you to leave Hawaii. I want you to stay. If we meet at this time tomorrow, about when I get off work, will you go home with me—leave the Korean and leave what he demands of you? Just being you and me?"

"If I go home with you, will your brothers and uncles gang bang me the way you said they did with Akamai?"

"No, of course not. It would be just you and me. I promise."

Tyler maintained a smile on his face, even though it wasn't the answer he was fishing for.

"We'll see what tomorrow brings," he said.

"Think about it. Think of what we can have together here. Think of me coming home to you every night and it just being the two of us."

After Lopaka left, to go off shift for the night, Tyler thought about the proposal.

* * * *

8:00 p.m.

Tyler was hanging over the side of the Jacuzzi in the German's hotel room, his knuckles dragging the wet marble floor, his heard lifted, eyes focused through the bathroom door to the hotel room beyond, his mouth set in a silent scream, as Gerhard, wearing surgical gloves, reamed his ass with four fingers up to the knuckles. Tyler had had to wear a skull cap after all. They both were wearing condoms too, and when Tyler sucked off the German, admonished not to touch the German anywhere but with his mouth on the cock, he had to do it through the film of a condom. Tyler was wearing a condom when the German jacked him too.

Tyler heard the sloshing of the water in the tub and sighed as the hand was withdrawn, but then the German was crouched over him, reaching around him with both hands—not touching him with them—to grip the edge of the Jacuzzi, as the German penetrated Tyler's ass and started to pump him. Tyler lowered his head, grimaced, and took the cocking.

They had started in the tub, facing each other, playing with each other's genitals with their feet. It was the closest they were to come to touchy feely, flesh on flesh.

Later a plastic sheet had been placed on the carpet in the bedroom. A footstool was on top of that, covered by a white sheet. Tyler was bent over the footstool, his groin pressed right at the top of the footstool and his torso hanging over the front, held in suspension by his arms stiff armed to the carpet. His legs were bent and pressing the footstool on both sides, his toes pressed into the carpet.

Crouched over him, not touching Tyler any more than inside his passage, with the cock, The German was rocking back and forth, pumping his way to another ejaculation.

At the door, still not touching Tyler anywhere, the German said the young man had done very well.

"I am pleased."

At 10:00 p.m. in Song Rhee's suite, the Korean was manhandling Tyler on the bed. The skull cap was off, and Rhee was touching Tyler everywhere. He was giving Tyler a pounding missionary, crouched between the young man's spread and bent legs, holding Tyler's torso arched back with an arm embracing the small of his back. Tyler's head was arched back too, his long, blond hair—the only hair on his body for now—was cascading down to the surface of the bed, jerking and shimmering to the rhythm of the long, fast slide inside him. Rhee fucked the shit out of the rent-boy.

At 11:00 p.m. Tyler lay in the bed on his back, panting and watching Rhee dress.

"I'm going out for a while. That was good. Fucked you good."

At 3:00 a.m. Tyler was awakened by the swaying bed. Rhee was fucking the young guy Tyler had seen Doug and Ray fuck in the bushes at the pool earlier that day. The young guy's face was turned to Tyler giving him mixed expressions of fright, horror, and passion. He no doubt had never had a cock as big and long as the Korean's inside him before.

At 4:00 a.m. the young man was lying on his back, moaning, beside Tyler. Tyler's chest was on the bed and his tail was in the air. Rhee was mounted on his ass, fucking him in long, deep strokes.

Tyler was aware that most young men would shrivel up when faced with the life of a high-priced rent-boy. But he wasn't most young men. And he loved the variety and frequency of the cocking. He'd liked the wildness of the Hawaiian middle-aged stud, he melted to the commanding dominance and huge cock of the Korean master. He even found interest in the antiseptic taking of the German fanatic. It was worthy of thought. He moved his head over to the young man's face, he was lying beside him and looking like he was lost in a crowd. They kissed, and he could feel the young man tremble. He also could . . .

At 4:30 a.m. Tyler was on top of the young man Rhee had brought back, kneeling between his thighs, embracing him close, and fucking him deep. Tyler had a very nice cock himself. The two beautiful young men were rocking against each other. The young man's torso was arched back, his eyes focused on the headboard, and he was moaning deeply. The Korean was stretched out beside them, watching them. He was stroking himself with one hand and squeezing and guiding one of Tyler's butt cheeks in the rhythm of the fuck. Rhee changed his position, rising up, mounting himself over Tyler's ass, penetrating him, and taking over the rhythm of the fucking of both cocks with his thrusts.

So much for day five of the Aloha week.

"Out of bed and pack. Our plane leaves in three hours."

"Our plane leaves today?" Tyler asked, coming out of a sensual doze, sitting up in the bed, and stretching. The young man from the previous night who, at some point Tyler learned was named Ted, had his head in Tyler's lap, giving him a blow job. Tyler gently pushed him away, and Ted reclined on the bed, played with his own cock, and both young men watched Song Rhee strut around the room, naked, his meat swinging free impressively, and throwing stuff in a suitcase.

"We have another day here, don't we?"

"Gerhard caved quickly—thank you for helping with that—and there's no use hanging around here for a day we don't need."

"We could enjoy just being in Hawaii," Tyler said, his mind racing on the possibilities that he could make it back out Lopaka's family's place—and that he could convince Lopaka to let his brothers and uncles truss him up and gang bang him. "There's an evening helicopter flight over all of the island that you could—"

"Don't worry, you'll get paid for the whole week," the Korean interjected. "I can use you on Guam as well as here. I'll keep you for the whole week."

Tyler shivered. He'd heard that Rhee had a sex torture chamber in his Guam house.

"I'm taking a shower," the Korean said. "Get dressed and pack. Not you," he said, pointing to Ted. "Want you again. Then you can get dressed and clear out. Your money's on the table over there."

"I need to get something at the pool that I left there," Tyler said, thinking fast. "The desk told me they'd found it, and it's at the pool desk."

"OK, do that and get back up here." He snapped his fingers at Ted, pointed to the bathroom, and headed in that direction.

As Tyler slipped on a Speedo, a T-shirt, and sandals, and looked around for whatever he didn't want to give up—including the $6,000 he found on the table, of course—and stuffing that into a backpack, he listened to the sounds of water running and sex. Rhee was fucking Ted in the shower and Ted was finding out all over again that Rhee could reach the back of his throat through his ass. Tyler shrugged and left the room.

He could only hope that Lopaka was on duty at the pool.

All the way down in the elevator, Tyler was still undecided. Go back to Guam with Song Rhee and enter the world of high-paid male hooker for as long as his looks held—be knocked about and treated like a slab of meat with his legs slapped open at the whim of some cruel rich slob. Or desert that life and Rhee and go home with Lopaka to face Lopaka's possessiveness—but his young, very nice cock.

When he got to the ground floor and walked out onto the pool terrace, Lopaka was just brushing past him and didn't see him. He quite evidently was following a man in his thirties who had a good face and a few extra pounds on him. The man looked around to ensure that Lopaka was following him. They took the path that would go by the garden room that Lopaka used to service the guests.

Feeling a flash of anger, Tyler turned and went back to the elevators. Who was Lopaka to dictate that Tyler would be exclusively for him while Lopaka continued fucking hotel guests for advantage and money? But then wasn't he, Tyler, scheming how he could have Lopaka and his brothers and uncles at the same time? And maybe what he saw didn't mean what he thought it did.

But it did mean that. Tyler veered away from the elevators and came back out to the pool and took the path around the building. When he reached the stand of foliage outside the patio door into the garden room, he saw the man on his back on the bed, legs spread and bent, and Lopaka between the man's legs, doing pushups on the man's ass. The man was holding Lopaka's slim hips between his hands. His head was lolled over toward the patio door, and there was a look of passion and complete satisfaction on his face.

At 2:00 p.m. the plane that Song Rhee and Tyler were in was taxiing away from the terminal at the Honolulu international airport. Tyler looked out and fancied that he saw Lopaka, only in the sarong he wore to give pool service at the Royal Hawaiian, running along the rail of the observation deck, waving at the airplane. Tyler pulled the window screen down and turned to pay attention to Rhee, who was already whispering in his ear what he planned to do with Tyler in the torture chamber under his house that night.

Tyler nodded his head and smiled. The Korean was fingering Tyler's basket.

~

About the Author

Habu is one of the pen names of a former supersonic spy jet pilot, intelligence agent, male model, movie actor, and diplomat. A wild youth in Southeast Asia was spent enjoying whatever sexual opportunities came his way, and much of his gay male writing is about recalling incidents from those days and inventing ones he'd perhaps have liked to experience. He now leads a very quiet and ordinary happily married family life.

An American, he is a published mainstream novelist and short story writer under another name and in another dimension of his life. He has written or cowritten (with Sabb) approaching 1,000 published short stories and over 100 published erotica e-books, primarily of gay fiction but also memoir, straight fiction and ménage fiction. His hand and creative writing can be seen in stories and books by habu, sr71plt, Dirk Hessian, Shabbu, and Stephen Kessel—among unrevealed others that might surprise readers. The fictionalized GM memoir *Flying High, Diving Deep* is loosely based on his life experiences. He can be found at the adults only gay male site www.BarbarianSpy.com, which he shares with Sabb and Dirk Hessian.

Our authors always like to receive feedback, and appreciate it when readers post reviews at distributors and other sites.

BarbarianSpy

FOR LITERARY HEAT

BarbarianSpy Books

Not all books listed below may currently be on release.
* indicates the book is available in paperback and e-book.

BOOKS BY CHRIS CROSS
Multisexual Adult Romance
Pulaski Square
Chocolate in Vanilla (MF)2
Christmas with Chris (MMF) (MM) (MF)

BOOKS BY ALEX LOCKHEED
Transgender Romance
Meeting Jenna
Transgender Other
Being Sarah

BOOKS BY DIRK HESSIAN
Xtreme Historical Erotica
Dirk's Ancient Times Collection (Print only Bundle)*
The King's Men
Shores of Tripoli*
Prophecy of Noto
Pretender's Fate
General Historical Erotic Romance
Dirk's America's Founding Collection (Print only Bundle)*
Soldier,Spy
Ridden West
Deliver a Virgin
Clouds and Rain
Confederate Gold
Puttin on the Ritz
To the Hessian Hills
Fire Down the Valley*
Constantinople*
The Beautiful Way*
Blue and Gray
Colonel's Treasure
Beginning of Time
Labyrinth

BOOKS BY HABU
Gay Erotica
Memoir Faction

Flying High, Diving Deep*
Xtreme Erotica
Fist of Gold
Liaisons
Chain Gang Banged (Short Story)
Tramp Steaming*
Escape to Girne
Silas' Choice*
Last Call
Choke Hold
Apyko: The Greek Pimp
Visits of the Schlange
Second Coming: Emile La Cour Unleashed*
Vortex: Sacrificed by Curiosity*
Dark Angel Sounding *(in e-book & included in Sounding:Ultimate Control paperback)**
Sounding: Ultimate Control (*Print Only*)*
Sounding Five *(in e-book & included in Sounding:Ultimate Control paperback)**
Romance
Gift from the Sea
Shore Leave
The Aviators
Poison Pen
Need to be Needed
Key Westing (short)
Finding a New Sam
Bangkok Summer Seduction
The Photograph
Inevitable Case
Turn to Love
Rain Check
Built for Pleasure (Sci Fi)
Danny's Choice*
Pull of the Groove
Sugar n Spice Christmas
Friday Nights with Lenny (Christmas Romance)
Snowy, Snowy Nights (Christmas Romance)
Tank n Bull
Sail to the Sun
War Letters
Ravens Roost
Caribbean Cruise Top to Bottom
Arena Stage
Trading Partners (Valentine's Day)
Four Coins
Lower Than the Heart (Valentine's Day)

Brambleton
Finding Amnad
Platres Conclave
Other Novels/Novellas
Different Strokes
Switching Sides
Also Want to Thank
Ranger Guided
Key Westing
Syrian Ram
Temptation's Clutches*
Descent into Chaos
Escape to Girne
Journey Through Abilene
Harmony and Dissonance
Stallion Station
Racing With the Devil (espionage suspense)
Prepared in Cape Verdi
Gilded Cage
House on Park*
Anything for Ambition
Dance of the Ravishers
Hard Knocks U*
My Neighbor's Spa*
Man's Man: Tales of a High Priced Gay Hooker*
Trip Money
The Indian Doctor
Sailorboy
Home to Fire Island
Switching Sides*
Murder Mysteries
Retribution (Hardesty)
Snitches (Hardesty
Gotta Keep Trying (Hardesty)
All Fools Day Foolery (Mike Kavanagh)
Inevitable Case (Mike Kavanagh)
Vanishing Laura
Death on a Ping Pong Table
Clint Folsom Mysteries Compendium Volume 1*
Death to Blonds - Stolen Judgment (Clint Folsom Mystery)*
Clint Folsom Mysteries Compendium Volume 2*
Gay Erotica Anthologies
A Hell of a War*
Earth Cry*
Shunga
Habu's Christmas Balls
Eight in D*

DevilMENt
Silas' Choices*
Stallion Station (A Novella in Parts)
Eleven to the Dogs*
Fifty Seventy*
Spy Tails 001*
Spy Tails 002*
Doubled*
Doubled Again*
Tails in the Tropics*
Tails in the Med*
Tails in the West*
Rough Riders*
Grab Bag 1*
Grab Bag 2*
Grab Bag 3*
Grab Bag 4*
Grab Bag 5*
Grab Bag 6*
Grab Bag 7*
Grab Bag 8*
Grab Bag 9*
Grab Bag 10*
Grab Bag 11*
Grab Bag 12*
Grab Bag 13*
Beyond the Beaded Curtain*
The Sporting Life*
Fetish Galore!*
Literary Gay Erotica
Cairo Surrender*
The Handyman*
Homeward Bound
Journey to Mirage*
Bisexual/Menage/Multisexual Erotica
And Eat it Too
Two Men, One Woman*
Every Which Way
Summer of Denial
Death on a Ping Pong Table
Cruising Gigolo
13 Ways for Halloween
Luther*
The Indian Prince*
BOOKS BY SABB
Spanish Lovers
Driver Reliever

Hiring in Hollywood
The Legend of Holleystone Grange
Surprise Encounters*
She is He
Wrong Man
Loyal to his King
Barbarian Tales - Book One - Traveler's Tales*
Barbarian Tales - Book Two - Journeys Begin*
Barbarian Tales - Book Three - The Inheritance*
Barbarian Tales - Book Four - Road to Persepolis*
BOOKS BY SHABBU
The Forever Man
Two Chances
A Season in Galicia*
Blind Dates*
Velvet Interrogation
Finding Jason
Dirty Pool
Operation Black Jade
Cigars!*
Angel in the Barn
Gayly Complicated*
Despoiling David
The Tree of Idleness*
I Met a Man
Rough Road to Happiness
BOOKS BY KIM BLACK
Lesbian Romance
Transfixed on Tammie (F/T lesbian)
~